iRapture

Jason Sullivan

Published by Fire Tale Press, 2024.

This is a work of fiction. Similarities to real people, places, or events are entirely coincidental.

IRAPTURE

First edition. November 1, 2024.

Copyright © 2024 Jason Sullivan.

ISBN: 979-8227355348

Written by Jason Sullivan.

Table of Contents

The Porcupine Fish Robbery 1
The Crabfood Nebula 7
Hysterica 12
Don't You Believe Me? 22
Writer Accused & Tank Writer 38
Flash Fiction Stories: Technology 48
Flash Fiction Stories: Pathos 61
Flash Fiction Stories: Dystopia 88
Children of the Veil 104
The Gung-Gung Tree 125
Wicker Aesthetics 131
The Two Million Year Cursmudge 136
Last Run of the Day 138
Acknowledgments 149
About the author 150

dedication

To my friends

epigraph

"Is all that we see or seem but a video game within a video game?" ~apologies to Edgar Allan Poe

Fire Tale Press

Libera verbum, libera animam.

Cover designed with Canva.

The Porcupine Fish Robbery

CHIEF WAS WORRIED. Were exotic fish robbers trying to steal his prize winning porcupine fish? He sat in his van, wearing his red top hat that the kids at his speaking engagements loved. Because he was tall, his friends had given him the nickname "Chief" after his favorite basketball player. He also had on the Chief's kelly green double zero basketball jersey. He needed to get to his talking gig. It was helping him pay for his PhD in oceanology. Unfortunately, a couple of potential exotic fish robbers had been trailing him when his van fishtailed, spilling most of the water from the tank. The men that had been following him pulled up next to his van in the parking lot. They both wore sunglasses and were dressed in gray jumpsuits. On the outside of the van, the sign read, "Exclusive Dealers in Exotic Fish". No need to be paranoid. Coincidences happen. Next to them, another van pulled up. This one read, "Locked out of your car? Call us!" That decided it. He would have to take the fish with him. This meant removing it from its traveling tank, which was mostly devoid of water at this point anyhow. He reached for his elbow length, triple thick, rubber gloves. He would have to get back to the van in less than three minutes and get the fish under water again. No problem. He could do it. He just needed to slowly jog while holding a prize winning porcupine fish. SLAP! SLAP! The gloves were on. He kicked open the back door and jumped out.

There he was, a man wearing a bright red top hat, basketball t-shirt, number 00, black rubber gloves up to his elbows, and white slacks with Conversational sneakers, and holding a two and a half foot long porcupine fish! An old lady entering the parking lot, in a VW bug, saw this aquatic oddity and drove right into a pole. Chief started to jog. He passed two teenagers in a convertible whose jaws dropped in unison at the sight of a large needled fish carried by a strange jogger. Their tongues popped out in shock, but were quickly retracted! He passed three nuns on the sidewalk. The nuns looked at the fish and then up to heaven. After the nuns, he stepped in a pothole, tripping slightly. He righted himself while holding Poky above his head, almost bringing the stabby fish down on top of an officer on patrol. Great, now he had an escort. A man came out of the convenience store lighting a cigarette. He casually noticed the spiny fish and crazy guy coming his way, "Hey, hold the door, will ya?" requested Chief. The cigarette guy managed to kick the door back in the nick of time, allowing the red top-hatted oceanologist-in-training to run by, and then Chief disappeared into the dark shade of the store.

"Barbecue or sour cream and onion? Barbecue or sour cream and onion? Barbecue or crazy person holding fish with giant thorns!" Ed had no time to make the choice which had moved from one of taste bud entertainment to one of life and death. He pulled the extra large bag of sour cream and onion potato chips off the rack and placed it between himself and the oncoming sticky fish train. The collision was immediate. The bag provided little protection, but it did pop magnificently as the spines continued through to the greasy t-shirt, after which there was nothing but fleshy belly. Thankfully, the momentum had decreased ever so slightly and the spines did not go in, too far. Poky stared with his great big fish eyes, first at the belly, and then at Chief, as if to say, "Why me?" He (the fish) was looking a little winded. "Shoot!" Chief yelled, and the policeman, who was only a few feet behind and had observed all this, pulled his gun. Chief didn't have time for in-depth explanations. He pulled Poky, releasing him from the potato chip man's spare tire. Chief sputtered out by way of explanation, "This fish needs water," and then he headed to the counter, where the best beef jerky in town awaited him in a jar next to the register.

The cashier had not failed to notice the collision. Perhaps it was the screams from the potato chip man. Now as a convenience store cashier, Tabo was no stranger to hold-ups. He had been in several, some of which he had successfully thwarted with his trusty Louisville slugger. For this one, however, he wasn't even going to try. Firstly, he was an animal lover and certainly did not want to smash a fish. Secondly, he had seen a lot of crazy things and this topped them all, so he just hit enter and the register draw sprang open. Ding! At just about this time, Chief threw the fully inflated porcupine fish down onto the artistically warn counter. It looked like a Jackson Pollock made out of illegible ink scrawl and permanently embedded gum smears. Several of Poky's spines stuck right in. The porcupine fish looked around the cash wrap with his big eyes. They came to rest on a bright yellow stack of Juicy Fruit gum. The cashier immediately started to fork the money over, but Chief yelled, "No, this isn't a robbery! I just need water for Pok ... the fish!" The cashier glanced at the fish dripping on his counter. It wore a sour cream and onion potato chip, speared by a spike above his right eye, like one of those little umbrellas you get with exotic drinks. He looked at the bleeding customer, who had chips sprinkled on his shoulders like a bad case of dandruff, then at the cop, whose gun was drawn and pointing in his direction, but at the fish! Chief noticed, too, and shouted at the policeman, "Don't shoot the fish!" The officer fired, and the cashier hit the ground, pulling at the drawer on his way down, catapulting the bills from the register into the air. Luckily for everyone, Sergeant Friendly was a professional and had merely fired a warning shot above the fish's head.

Chief grabbed some water and some jerky. It was the best in town! He threw a few bills from his wallet onto the counter. Then, after taking a quick look around the store at the fresh bullet hole in the window behind the counter, the bloody chip man, a cop on the floor pointing a gun at him, the assorted customers hiding behind candy bar racks, and some dude trying to crawl into the two-inch space below the freezer, he decided to throw in a few more bucks for the damages. He thought this was generous because it wasn't his fault everyone had freaked out. Well, maybe it was a little.

He had to get back to his van, and quickly! Unfortunately, in the small convenience store, there was only one way out, and that was the way he had come in. He grabbed the water with one hand and Poky with the other, beef jerky in mouth, and started to run. Sergeant Friendly saw two pairs of eyes coming right at him. He was not a coward, and he was rather upset at this spiky fish robber, but all he could think of was his son's aquarium and all the little fish, and he would never be able to explain to his boy why he had shot a fish, and, of course, there was also the realization that if he shot the alleged spiky fish robber and his spiky menace the inertia would land them right on top of him. So just as Chief and the fish were leaping over the potato chip man, the sergeant turned sideways to let them pass. Chief could not believe his good luck. He turned his head and said to the policeman, with beef jerky in his mouth, "Hurmph, tunks mun!" and in the process, the beef jerky fell. He knew not where.

When he turned around, a split second later, he was hopping up the steps to the school bus that had just pulled in front of the store and opened its door to unload children. "Wow! Where'd this come from?" he exclaimed in dire earnestness. The lady driver had, in another split second, climbed up behind the wheel, which she did not technically have to do because Chief was able to make the corner and start running down the aisle. The children, many of whom only an instant before were standing in the aisle anticipating de-busing, being young and agile, easily (more or less) dived back into their seats. One notebook was dislodged in the process, causing papers to fly everywhere, and, of course, Poky picked one up, this time with the spine over his left eye. Chief ran out through the emergency exit and was quite proud of himself because those kids had probably never seen a fish like Poky.

He was home free. He just had to get past the crowd that had gathered to watch, as well as the back-up police cars with their doors open with cops hunkered behind them aiming their guns at him, but wait, someone yelled, "He's got a hostage!" and all the cops dropped their guns. What was this about a hostage? Did they mean Poky? No, evidently while he was on the bus, some kid had jumped on his back in the commotion and was still clinging. Chief was upset and frankly, insulted, at all the names he was being called, first "robber" and now "hostage taker", still he needed to get Poky into some water fast, so as the crowd and police parted like the Red Sea for Moses, he briefly explained, "Hey, just saving a fish, people!" Chief placed the kid, who actually seemed to be enjoying the ride, Poky having calmed him with his big fish eyes, next to the nearest officer, and proceeded to jump into the van whose back doors were still open. He quickly poured the water into the tank, not enough to fill it but it would do, and threw Poky back in. There was enough salt in there so Poky would be OK for a while. He ripped off his gloves and revved the van. Too bad he had dropped the beef jerky, because he really needed it after all that. But there it was, stuck on one of Poky's spines! He reached back and grabbed it. Ouch! The blood was pouring. He had caught his finger on a spine. Not a problem, a little blood on the beef jerky. Everything is cool. Then over the curve, carefully avoiding those three nuns by at least an inch, and finally, off to the aquarium. There was no immediate police pursuit. Chief chuckled to himself, "What are they going to do, charge me with assault with a deadly porcupine fish!"

The Crabfood Nebula

OUTSIDE HIS SPACESHIP window were the delicious fuchsia pink-purple hues of the Crab Nebula. Framed by this enchanting backdrop were the mythological Singing Water Planets. Well, they weren't a myth anymore. Gerez the explorer had discovered them. Getting around the dark space anomaly was tricky. That was why he was alone on the trip, and there would be no contact with home until he managed the equally tricky return. But that was for later. For now, there was much to explore. Only one part of the myth remained to be proven. Did the exotic inhabitants of the Singing Water Planets exist? The stories described them in many ways, but almost all of them had one common adjective: spicy! Gerez would soon find out.

The towns reminded him of pictures of old fishing villages on Earth. The planet was mostly ocean but there were many sandbars, some of them miles across, and the Crabulans lived in beach shacks, extremely sophisticated, high-tech, beach shacks. Everywhere Gerez looked there were signs depicting the Crabulans, with their tiny eyes and snappy claws, floating about in pots. Well, actually, the "pots" were the Crabulan version of hot tubs. They loved relaxing in hot tubs. Sometimes the water was very hot, and they almost always added spicy bath salts. Gerez thought the salts mixing with the steam smelled just like that wonderful spice, Old

Chessie. It was driving him wild. It got so bad that he tried his best to avoid the Crabulan bath houses, crossing the street if necessary. He was afraid of what might happen if he followed his olfactory desires and hopped in a tub with some jumbos!

Gerez's guide to Crabula was a seven foot tall blue crab! Not a jumbo crab, a giant, humongous, larger than he was, crab! His name was Zander Crash. The Crabulans, since they had no vocal cords, used their claws to communicate. They would tap on each other's shells. With Gerez, Zander tapped on his space helmet. It was weird wearing it around, but hey, you make adjustments on deep space missions. Somehow Gerez understood what Zander was saying. Maybe it was some type of universal crab tapping language, but what he did not like was how Zander would hold him with his other claw while doing this. Sometimes he squeezed a little too hard.

After Zander came from the pots, he would smell of Old Chessie. This drove Gerez wild. He had not eaten any decent food since leaving Earth, and all they offered him to eat on Crabula was this strange mush that tasted like chicken. He did not like it at all, but crabs were his favorite food! Because of his location on Crabula, he was in a total communications blackout with Earth. He was on his own! And he could not help but think that maybe he could just eat one of them without anyone noticing. They smelled just like his favorite blue crabs from home, and they were so big, how could he resist? How could he pass up such a culinary opportunity? After all, it was becoming more and more apparent that achieving normalized relations with these aliens was highly unlikely. He, after all, was not the only Earthling that enjoyed blue crabs! So it was that he decided to chow down, that very night, after Zander had returned from the pots. Before anyone found out, he would quietly sneak off the planet and return home, telling the Space Board that conditions were far too tempting, or rather, dangerous in that area of the galaxy.

Meanwhile, as Zander soaked in the hot pots, he too had been thinking about what sort of space relations could take place between the two planets, Crabula and Earth. He smiled. He was afraid there was only one kind! He knew their visitor, Gerez, would have to be given a negative reply to his application for initial trade and social relations between the two worlds. He would be going home empty-handed, and yet, there was another way. Space accidents happened all the time, and if Gerez did not return from his deep space mission, chances were that the Earthlings would be very cautious before sending another spaceship. It was a politically tasty, ah, salient idea, he thought to himself. He had to go see Gerez to tell him the bad news. On the way out, he grabbed a jar of barbecue sauce, just in case,

They met at the sandbar where Gerez had first landed. Both seemed a little nervous, and neither could guess why the other one was acting strangely. Gerez had one hand behind his back, which was holding his improvised shellfish hammer. Sander had one hand behind his shell, holding a jar of barbecue sauce. He motioned to the dug-out crab lair nearby, for some privacy, of course. This was perfect as Gerez had some Old Chessie hidden there that he just happened to have on his ship. It was a joke gift for the trip! They scuttled in sideways, Zander having a definite advantage here, each keeping the one arm hidden. It was fairly dark inside the hollow, with only the lights from the beach illuminating the inside. Gerez could smell the aroma from the spicy pots on Zander. It was driving him wild. He tried to play it cool.

"Well, I think I should be leaving soon. I'm afraid I can't recommend a furthering of relations between our worlds," said Gerez, deeply breathing in the spicy scent.

"So soon?" responded Zander, as he gastronomically considered Gerez. "Oh, I think you are right. Earth and Crabula are not a good match. But won't you stay for one last meal?"

Gerez wondered why Zander was so eager to agree. The Earth always offered a very attractive Junior Trade Partner package, but it was hard to tell with aliens what their motives were. It was, after all, for the best. If and when the Crabulans found out they were a giant-sized Earth delicacy, they were sure to be offended. And who knew what some of the more opportunistic members of the board might propose? As for Zander's suggestion about a meal, that sounded great, because the spicy aroma drifting off the Crabulan was driving Gerez crazy! He could barely think straight. Gerez gripped his hammer more tightly and tried to maneuver behind Zander. He responded to the dinner invitation. "One more meal was just what I had in mind, and I'd love it to be you, ah, with Old Chessie, you know, spicy!" Strangely, Zander seemed to be matching him move for move. Gerez glimpsed the jar of barbecue sauce that Zander was holding behind his back. He figured it was probably for more of that disgusting chicken-tasting stuff that they ate. And the look in his eyes was truly one of a starved cat, but why was he so hungry? No matter, Gerez was hungry for a super jumbo crab. He lifted his mallet high, but before he could bring it down, he saw the strangest thing. It was a little eighteen-inch tall person running out of the hollow. He blinked twice, and it was gone.

"What was that?" he demanded of Zander.

Zander answered slowly, while opening his claw and easing it toward Gerez, "Oh that, that was a Humken."

"What are Humkens?" stuttered Gerez, suddenly having lost his appetite.

"Humkens are what we eat!" he said, making a quick grab for Gerez's neck with his claw.

Gerez ducked and ran for the beach, saying, "Oh my galaxy! That barbecue sauce was for me!"

His ship was not far, but the thought of these Crabulans feeding on Humkens filled him with horror. He said to himself, "If I ever get back, I'll never eat another crab cake!" With that, he jumped through the portal to his ship, made sure the hatch was secured, and was soaring skyward in under three minutes.

Zander watched from the beach with another Crabulan.

"Where's he going in such a rush?"

"He had to leave before he was ... ah, before dinner."

"I doubt civilized relations with jumbo Humkens could ever have been established." commented his friend. And then added, "Do you think we should follow his spaceship? After all, there are probably a lot of giant Humkens where he is headed!"

"I like the idea," said Zander, "but he left this little can of spices behind." He held up the Old Chessie canister. "These spices smell a lot like our bath salts." They stared at each other for a moment, contemplating the odd ways of the giant Humken. Zander then said, "Maybe we should just leave them alone." The watched as the spaceship disappeared into the sky and Zander said, "Let's go get some dinner. I brought the barbecue sauce!"

Hysterica

"HYSTERICA, I WANT YOU."

"I am coming. I am always coming. I will be your dutiful servant. But you cannot have me right now. I must finish cleaning the house."

And so it was with the orange cleaner, lemon cleaner, ammonia cleaner and a host of other cleaners. Her platinum blond hair and her polished blue eyes were always in motion. A goddess in disguise, she worked in bright clean clothes with a smile that was so pleasing, so receptive.

"Hysterica, I will see you tonight," said the Mr. in the suit. He did not even look at her as, with coffee and paper in hand, he zipped out of the kitchen. He had a lot on his mind. He was a man of standing and means with a family to provide for. She was less than nothing to him. Yet every fiber of his being ached for her, lived for her.

She shot a Jersey accented "Late-AH!" at his back, then froze for an instant with a Super Suds smile plastered across her face.

The boy, Jimmy, and girl, Susie, were next. They ran for the door, sugared cereal crumbs falling from their clothes. They would soon be with their friends, in school in the morning and on the soccer fields in the afternoon. They shouted "Bye" almost in unison before the door slammed shut behind them. She was nothing to them. But she was the gatekeeper to the excitement underlying everything, and they wanted access. They lived for her. She placed her bare forearm on the glass door, propping it open slightly while sticking her Super Suds smile through, and she yelled, "Late-AH."

At last she was alone with her cleaning products and her friends on TV. Her hair, beautifully white in the warmth of the morning sun, reflected a blinding sheen. The floor glistened, and the countertops glistened, and the toilet bowl glistened, but her pure white hair glistened most of all. And the utensils shined, and the glasses shined, and the windows shined, but her shallow blue eyes shined more than any of them. And she began to softly spin. One foot as the pivot, the other giving a gentle push. Slowly at first, the day had just begun.

Everyone collected Cosmic Coupons. It was what they did. Cosmic Coupons shot up from just about everything. They were the tangible rewards of interactivity in the form of waxy strips of paper. They each displayed a very exciting number, representing credits, alongside a wise saying. Cosmic Coupons were used in the Ritual, where they were turned in for all the things a person could ever want. The Cosmic Coupons came out of cellphones, computers, parking meters, the desks at school, cash registers, and all other manner of contrivance. No button could be pushed without a waxy credit coupon issuing forth. The more you pushed, the more Cosmic Coupons you got. It was that simple. It was quite possible, however, to push all day and still not get a high number. The numbers ranged from one to one thousand. Most were under a hundred and a day when a number over a hundred was received was a very special day indeed. When a high number was grabbed, it was hard to get through the day for thinking of the excitement to come.

At Sure Fire elementary, the teacher asked questions, and the students selected the answers on the screens on their desks. For each one right, they received a Cosmic Coupon. Jimmy was hot today. He had collected about two dozen already, but nothing with a very high number. Then he got a thirty-five. He smiled. He was not sure, but that might be enough to get what he wanted that evening. It filled him with excitement thinking about it.

After dinner, it was time for the Ritual. Jimmy, Suzie and the Mr. gathered around Hysterica in the den. The large screen TV was on in the background, as it always was. This did not bother them in the least. It added atmosphere. Hysterica stood up and walked to the middle of the floor. She wore a sleeveless red blouse and a white canvas dress cut just below the knees. On her feet, she had blue sneakers. With her right foot, she gave the initial push off the carpeted floor. Then, slowly at first, she spun.

Jimmy threw down at her feet a coupon with the number fifteen. He shouted the wise saying, "Work hard, live long." And made his request, "Fifteen is for a video game!"

Hysterica twirled a little faster.

Suzie threw a coupon with the number twelve, and yelled, "Fame makes better people of us all. Twelve is for an MP3 player!"

And Hysterica spun faster. Pushing with her right foot, her perfect blond hair falling to one side. The Mr. threw in a coupon, he shouted, "Buying is good for you and your country." And his wish, "Seven is for a new TV!"

They all began throwing Cosmic Coupons, yelling the number of credits and stating their desired object. Each tried to out yell the other until the screaming and the coupon tossing became loud and frantic. Hysterica began to spin rapidly. She had a faraway look in her eyes and her arms undulated with the twirling. The Mr.,

Jimmy and Suzie swung their arms more desperately, like swimmers in a fifty-meter dash. Waxy Cosmic Coupons littered the floor at Hysterica's swiftly spinning feet. All of a sudden, Jimmy threw in his thirty-five and yelled, "Thirty-five for video game!" He followed with the saying, "Stuff will never let you down." Hysterica screamed at the top of her lungs, "Jimmy's video game!" She screeched to a halt and collapsed onto the carpet. The family bowed their heads in respect. Jimmy would get his video game. It was waiting for him in his room. She had made it so.

Jimmy skulked off to his room with a big smile on his face. He felt special, oh so excited, and only a little ashamed. The family looked at the red in Jimmy's cheeks as he went to be alone with his video game. It was what he wanted so badly, what he needed. The rest of them watched TV and were happy. Perhaps Hysterica would give them what they wanted tomorrow evening. As for Hysterica, they never thought that she might want something, might need something. She was less than nothing to them and yet she was everything. They lived for her.

Hysterica had all the MakeBelieve line of cosmetics. She wanted to be beautiful, she had to be beautiful. MakeBelieve Cosmetics made her so. She got up an hour before anyone else and sat in front of the bright lights of her makeup mirror. Everything had to be perfect. Her makeup, her clothes, her weight. Every part of her said who she was, what she was good for, and how much she was loved. In the afternoon, after she had cleaned all morning, she would have a diet bar and pore through catalogs. Every piece of clothing had to be just right. Beauty was not an option, it was her identity. She needed to be wanted, she lived to be wanted. And she was only a shell, less than nothing, but she was also the matrix for everything a body could want. In the afternoon, the twirling came easier, helped by the growing pathos.

Susie enjoyed walking home from school with her cellphone. She had lots of people to call, but she mostly spoke with her friend, Sally. Sally was very hip. She had all the cool stuff, even if she tended to talk too fast and breathe even faster. Susie always liked to add to the Cosmic Coupons she had accumulated during school by making several calls on the way home. After she made her third call in five minutes, she was rewarded with an awesome coupon. It had the number eighty-seven on it. It said, "Need never fails to feed." She knew all about that. She thought she would be getting that MP3 player tonight for sure. She immediately told her friend. Sally squeaked and wanted to hang up so she could call her back. Sally needed new gold earrings. Unfortunately, Sally kept hanging up as soon as Susie would answer just so she could call again and get another coupon. She really needed those earrings. "Take it easy," warned Susie. But it was too late. Sally had contracted a common malady known as Multipushphoria. Susie ran around the block to find Sally lying on her back, kicking her feet in the air and, with a mesmerized look on her face, madly calling on her cellphone over and over again. She couldn't stop. Cosmic Coupons were pouring out at a rapid clip, but Sally was too far gone to notice. Susie called the medics, who came and took her friend away. "Button pushing is good," this was the message on the one thousand credit coupon, but Multipushphoria did create problems from time to time. "Is she going to be OK?" Susie asked.

"Oh yeah, she just needs a healthy dose of a sedative. Would you like to come along and stay with your friend until she feels better?" the medic asked.

"No, I got an eighty-seven," said Susie as she turned and headed for home.

"Sorrow disappears at the mall. Twenty-seven! I want game controllers!" yelled Jimmy as he threw the waxy paper at Hysterica's feet.

The evening's ritual had just begun. Suzie read the coupon, "To the good the spoils go." And chimed in, "Thirty-five. I want an MP3 player." With hunger in her eyes, Suzie watched Hysterica spin. She was hypnotized by her movements and obsessed with her beauty. One day she would spin like Hysterica, but not tonight. She was still all need, all want. There was nothing more beautiful in the world than Hysterica spinning. Susie had to have what she knew everyone wanted. What she knew only Hysterica could give to her. Thinking about it made her want the MP3 player even more.

"Twenty. I want a new TV," yelled the Mr. and, before throwing in his coupon, he recited, "A broke neighbor is no friend indeed."

Hysterica's speed was increasing. Her hair reached out towards them. "Twelve. I need new game controllers," shouted Jimmy. His coupon read, "The more you have, the better."

It was Susie's turn again, and to everyone's surprise, she yelled out, "Eighty-seven! I need an MP3 player!" Shock hung on the Mr. and Jimmy's faces. Hysterica started to spin madly before throwing her head back and shouting, "Susie shall have an MP3 player!" She then collapsed to the floor. The others bowed their heads in respect.

Suzie was elated. She felt giddy. Until she grew up and took on the role herself, she still had the right to want. She still needed things from the font of all excitement, the mediator of the good products. Her MP3 player would be in her room and she would go to it. It was just what she wanted, always wanted. With only a slightly embarrassed smile and expectation in her eyes, she disappeared into her room. The others watched TV.

The cars, the jewelry, the houses, the club memberships, these were the cornerstones of Hysterica's existence. Like a chess master, she handled her pieces adeptly. The others would want what she wanted them to, although they would think it their own secret desire. She would never say a word, but her twirling would tell them, and the TV would, too, and they would think the want, the need, to be their own. So it was that the Mr., Jimmy and Susie pushed through another day. In their shiny car past the expensive houses to the school by the park or the building by the other building. Everything was theirs, or someone's, to possess. But the matrix was the want. She was the center. Through her, it all came.

The Mr. pushed the elevator button for the seventh floor and instinctively grabbed his Cosmic Coupon from the eCaus coupon dispenser on the wall of the elevator. While checking the credits, almost unconsciously out of the corner of one eye, he thought about how during the last several nights he had not gotten what he needed. Maybe tonight would be the night. His new Cosmic Coupon displayed the number one hundred and thirteen, "Wanting is the foundation of being." No one had to tell him that. He would get his tonight. Suddenly, the elevator eCaus began to convulse. It looked like it was going to explode. Bam! It started to spaz, spitting Cosmic Coupons everywhere. Every once in a while, the eCaus machines would become overwhelmed and throw up in everyone's face. The people in the elevator were jumping all over the place, grabbing at the fluttering pieces of waxy paper, trying to collect as many Cosmic Coupons as possible. The Mr., however, got off at the next floor. He had his number, and it was a good one. No need to act like an idiot anymore for the rest of the day.

That evening, as he sat near the spinning feet of Hysterica, he was awestruck by her beauty. He was every night. Whether he got what he wanted or not, the magic of Hysterica always lifted his spirits. As an adult, he knew, unlike the kids, that it was not the getting that was important. It was the wanting. To want Hysterica so, to see her beauty, to feel her each night lift the world up off the ground and keep it there afloat, gravityless, for all to desire, for all to crave. This was what life was about. As her blouse fluttered in the dance, he glimpsed the curve of her breast giving with the press of the spin, the sweat glistened on her neck, just the right amount, and her "breath-stopping" platinum blond hair, pure and clean, pulled them all into the excitement. He loved her more than he would ever be able to understand, and she was less than nothing. He threw down his coupon. "One hundred and thirteen for a new TV!"

Hysterica let out a groan and, in a shattered voice, yelled, "The Mr. will get his TV tonight!" then she collapsed to the floor. They all bowed their heads in respect.

As he proudly stepped off to the bedroom, he was more satisfied than any man could ever be. He had it all. Life was very good. To get what you want and to be able to spend time with it alone, what more could anyone ask for? Hysterica gave him and his family what they wanted, what they needed. As he shut the door to the bedroom, he felt satisfied, deeply satisfied. Hysterica sat down with the kids to watch TV, and in a voice that was surprisingly cheery so soon after the exhausting ritual, she said, "I love you." They knew she did. They had the stuff in their rooms to prove it.

Late that night, as the family slept the sound sleep of the just benefited, Hysterica opened her eyes. She quietly slipped out of bed and into the shadowy hallway. She walked through the living room. Glancing into the den, she half expected to see the Ritual still happening, but it was eerily silent. Only darkness sat in the circle by the TV. She moved through the kitchen, opened the door and stepped out into the backyard. The grass felt like waxy Cosmic Coupons beneath her feet. She laid down, leaning her head against one of the plastic yard toys.

She looked towards the stars in the sky. Thousands of them, bright gems of light in a heather gray sky, but the gold speckles on her new amber refrigerator were all that she could see. She started to breathe faster. But there was no air to be had, not even in the sky. The void mercilessly sucked all the products from her mind. She grabbed at a plastic pail. She would not let it go. She would hold on to this thing so that no one could ever take it from her. But her fingers lost their strength. The terror was overwhelming. She could not resist it any longer. She turned herself inside-out so that every "thing" in her life was obliterated. It was just her, floating on one exquisitely shameful thought: she had been used by all the products, by her family and her society. Her people had taken everything from her, but they would not have the one last thing. It burned inside her, more beautiful than the prettiest diamond and more powerful than the biggest SUV. Jimmy, Susie and the Mr. would never possess it because no amount of coupons could call it forth. A few nights ago, when she first noticed it, a door had opened. She had entered with trepidation. Now she quickly, anxiously stepped through. It was so still. Nothing spun inside. She heard the strangest sound. It was her own voice telling her to shut the door. She knew if she shut the door, she could never go back.

How could she leave Jimmy, Susie, and the Mr.? She peered up at their windows. They would be asleep dreaming of products to come. Her family was everything to her and they were less than nothing. As she shut the door, she heard herself whispering, "Late-AH!"

Don't You Believe Me?

"WELCOME TRAVELER, WELCOME to Placia," said a tall, lithe man, wearing sky blue linen of the finest weave, as he beckoned me towards the lights below. He was not disturbed by my disheveled appearance, nor by what must have been the crazed look in my eyes. This time, this place, was far out of sync with my time. I knew this. But it was not as if I had traveled through time. No, it was not like that. This was part of my life, my destiny, a destiny that is ours together as humans. Still, each step I put on the pebbled road into Placia seemed unreal, impossible. There was a breeze blowing that night. A gentle, warm breeze coming off the sea, flickering the many torches and candles lighting the streets. Placia had wide streets, open courtyards and an inviting square. This ease was also reflected in the manner and dress of the inhabitants. As we walked through the streets, I wanted to ask him his name, but I never found the right moment. He never asked me about mine as he seemed to know who I was or, at least, why I was there. As we entered the spacious town square, paved with an intricate blue and white mosaic, many of the townspeople gathered around us. They, too, were tall and lithe and had a lightness about their being. They looked upon me with the interest of those engaged in a complex game and I was a new clue. At last, I found words and asked, "Is this Rome or Greece?" At first, the Placians did not seem to know what to make of this. Then they all burst into a frolicking laughter. My guide responded with a kind smile, "No ... no, you are not in Rome ... or Greece." That evening and the following days were the most idyllic in my life with the exception of one moment. I am now so distant from that place, here in a world filled with toil and distress. But I tell you the magic of Placia is here as well, active each day, if it could only be uncovered. If we could undo the work of that thing, I first met there.

I thought Placia a heaven on earth. The Placians, however, spoke of an even more wonderful time. The ease, beauty and wisdom with which the Placians lived was something to be admired. I say ease not because they were rich, or lazy, but because their actions were in harmony with each other and their surroundings. There was little stress. The Placians were skilled artisans, elegant pottery, and mosaics adorned their streets and houses. They were skilled horticulturists with healthy plants and trees, full crops and remedies for every imaginable ailment. Although some excelled in certain activities, they jealously guarded the right to take part in them all, as if to be restricted from an endeavor would lessen an individual.

It was within this serene environment that a most disturbing development took place. There was a renowned teacher among them who taught the brightest of their sons and daughters. I was lucky enough to hear him teach on one occasion. He had the ability to reach inside students and encourage their thirst for knowledge on a profound level. He would sometimes reference the Old Ones, a group of people who existed before the Placians. One day, while the town was holding a meeting in the square, a chill wind curved its way around the ornate pottery, slid over the tiled square and, in a sudden violent departure, almost extinguished the torches and candles lighting the town. I did not know it at that time, but the Cloaked Diminisher had swept through. There was silence. Then an unsettled rustle spread through the crowd of Placians.

Suddenly, a Placian stood up and, with a look of banality on his face, he proclaimed, "I do not want the wise one teaching my son anymore. The wise one's ideas make him think of things other than Placia. I do not see how this can benefit us. He must stop."

Another stood up, "I agree. The wise one must be driven away. He does not seem content to teach the rules of Placia but wanders into dangerous ideas, often about the Old Ones."

One of the kindest and most refined of the women stood up. "What are you saying? He is our best teacher. The ways of the Old Ones are the foundation for our way of life."

"Silence sympathizer!" a low and mean voice from deep within the crowd demanded. "Do not speak against your people. He must go. The will of the people has spoken. On the third day, he will be summoned to this square, and the pronouncement made." A hush fell over the square and the Placians slowly began to disperse into the cold night air. I was shocked. Placia did not seem like the place where I had first arrived. Something had changed. I would later find out the Cloaked Diminisher had enacted the change.

Over the next three days, a small group of Placians formed in support of the wise teacher. I joined them, but as discreetly as possible as I was concerned about what seemed to be a growing hatred toward this wise member of the Placian community. I was confused and wanted answers, so I went to see the Placian prognosticator.

"What is going on?" I asked. "Why has such a wise and generous community turned on its greatest teacher?"

It was then that I first heard its name spoken. The prognosticator replied, "It is the Cloaked Diminisher. It found us in the square. We were not ready for it and in that second we were defeated." He paused, looking toward the sky before continuing, "Placia will go on to be in many ways greater than it is now. It will become a rich and powerful land before it is destroyed. However, what took place yesterday was the pivotal battle. And in our defeat is sealed the downfall of our civility."

"What is this thing, this Cloaked Diminisher?" I asked. "How could such a terrible event take place so quickly and without any warning?"

"I cannot answer your question completely. The Old Ones lived for many, many generations before the Cloaked Diminisher. From somewhere it emerged and in so doing ended the time of the Old Ones. Among those Placians capable of understanding the Cloaked Diminisher, many thought that it had only affected the Old Ones and that it was now gone forever. I recently spoke of this with the wise teacher. We were concerned that this was not the case and that the Cloaked Diminisher would return to continue to force humanity downwards. We thought it might well be close even as we spoke. We weren't sure how to protect ourselves and our people. We did not know how to fight it. If the Old Ones had been brought down by it, what chance did we stand? I thought we had more time but now it falls to the next level. As if moving underground to lower and lower levels, we descend into the darkness it brings. I must go. I have much to do. Good luck, my friend." As he placed his hand on my shoulder, I was pushed forward. I was not there to see what happened to the wise teacher. I would later find out, but only after arriving in a much different place.

It was St. Echinops day and everyone was celebrating. It was the third saint's day this week and there was no work being done. I met Echibar at the edge of the village square. His hoop sprang right into my hands. Surprised, I held on to it. All manner of game was being played in the square, along with dancing and music.

"A happy St. Echinops Day to you, my friend! Are you not playing a game? What fun are you having today?"

I was somewhat taken aback by his question and responded with hesitation, "I am a visitor."

"Well, all the more reason you should celebrate. What is your game of preference?"

"Ah, you know, whatever. The hoop looks like fun."

"A man after my own heart. It is great fun. You look like you have left your hoop in ... where is it you said you are from? No matter, I will get you another one and some grog. You'll feel merrier with some grog in you!"

Echibar fetched me a hoop, a stick and some grog and before I knew it, I was having a great time caught up in the festivities. I was not as good as Echibar, but I tried to keep up, often having to grab my hoop. Many of the villagers looked at me with concern in their eyes, but after they saw I was with Echibar, they relaxed and accepted me wholeheartedly into their festivities. I asked Echibar, "Why the look of worry when they see me?"

"Everyone is a little wary of strangers. It is rumored there are witches about, although no one has actually seen one."

At the edge of the festivities, I noticed a man who appeared, by his clothes and his countenance, to be of some importance. He had noticed me also and was gesturing for me to come over.

"You better go," said Echibar. "Nobody denies the doctor." He added with a smile, "If he wants to use his tools on you, invoke the name of St. Echinops and it may gain you another day."

Not knowing if I would see him again, I nodded thankfully to Echibar. I headed for the doctor whose name I would learn was Dr. Minstreldame.

"Greetings. I am glad you have arrived during the festivities of St. Echinops. The people of this village are, for the most part, good people and it is best to see them on a saint's day when they are joyous."

We walked back to his house, that was a half-mile or so outside of the village. It was a fair-sized house with fields of rye growing around it. He showed me into his study, an open room with a wide central window, plaster walls, and wood beams. Hanging on the walls were drying herbs. Scrolls were piled high upon the shelves. To one side was a large table, next to which sat many somewhat frightening looking instruments. At the far end was a desk covered with scrolls, some opened to particular passages. He gestured to a seat by the window for me, and he sat down in an ornate wooden chair across from it. He inquired, "Can I get you something to eat or drink?"

I had some food during the festival, so I declined his offer. He smiled.

"Is this France during the Dark Ages?" I suddenly asked, almost surprising myself.

"France? The 'dark' ages?" he responded, puzzled. "No … no, you are not there. It is not a perfect age, but darkness does not prevail, although it may be gaining in power. I fear your arrival confirms this."

Feeling somewhat unsettled at my failure to identifying my surroundings, and uneasy at what unpleasant event the doctor seemed to associate with me, I pleadingly responded, "I assure you, I mean no harm. I am merely a traveler on a journey which, I must confess, I know not how it began nor where it will end."

"I do not fear you. I fear the Cloaked Diminisher. I fear what it will do to my time and my people."

The mention of the Cloaked Diminisher cast a pall upon the room. Our eyes met. For the first time, I felt as if we understood each other. I was not afraid. I did, however, feel sorry that my journey was continuing. I was also concerned about what this meant for the good people of this place and time.

"I have worked my whole life so that this day may never happen. Nevertheless, here it is. Although I dread the arrival of the Cloaked Diminisher, your presence here means there is still hope, even if less hope, for another time and place."

He gently lifted a hand to his face as he looked out upon his place in history. He knew that very soon it would change forever. Mustering what spirit he could, the doctor continued, "I will tell you what I know. What has passed since your last encounter with the Cloaked Diminisher?"

"After you left Placia, they banished the wise teacher. The legacy of the Cloaked Diminisher initially helped the Placians become very rich and powerful. However, eventually it encouraged them to turn on each other. This infighting led to their downfall. After Placia, huge civilizations arose, built upon the backs of slaves. The power of these societies lay in their ability to obtain and control slaves. This was how it was until the time of Liberus. Liberus encouraged slaves to struggle for their freedom. The slave-based societies hunted the rebellious slaves down, destroyed them at every opportunity. Even so, many were inspired by Liberus and dared to set out to control their own destiny."

"It was then that the Cloaked Diminisher had its supreme moment of glory. It twisted Liberus's message. The people began to think that Liberus had freed the slaves forever, no matter what anybody did or how they might act. The Cloaked Diminisher placed this twisted thought in the minds of men: slaves could remain in slavery and still be free. The largest civilization the world has ever known arose with this pivotal deceit as its foundation. There were more slaves than ever, but they saw themselves as free because Liberus had 'freed' them. When, in actuality, they had been tricked out of their freedom by the Cloaked Diminisher. However, even this powerful empire based upon 'freed' slaves would eventually fall. Over the centuries, the Cloaked Diminisher eroded the empire's strength until it was no longer capable of holding off the growing tide of barbarism."

"There appear to be levels, you see, like rungs on a ladder descending into a well, each level darker than the last. There was the time of the Old Ones, then the ancients, followed by the great time of slavery, then barbarism and, now, this time. In each time the Cloaked Diminisher has taken something foundational from us, from all of humanity, and replaced it with a hollow shell, a mere contrivance. Even worse, there seems to be a cumulative effect. With each fall, another light within us loses its brightness. In each period, we have less capacity to fight for that which makes us human than we did in the previous one."

"In our time, through the dishonesty and greed of the villagers, the lords have arisen. Using the fear inspired by the Cloaked Diminisher, they have promised to protect the people, but only if the people pledge obedience. I felt something had to be done to restore the trust and vision of the Old Ones before the Cloaked Diminisher struck again. I thought the answer lay in keeping the people happy, the joyous celebrations of the saints' days, the games and festivities. The lords, however, saw the people growing less fearful and, with this, their loyalty starting to wane. To increase the public fear and strengthen their power, the lords started to spread rumors of evil witches hiding among us, waiting to jump out and steal our souls. I did not know what to do to combat this lie. Now you are here."

"Warlock! He is a warlock!" The villagers came shrieking down the lane. A crowd of townspeople had formed at the instigation of the local lord, and they were coming for Dr. Minstreldame.

"They don't know what they are doing," he said. "They are good people. You know this. You met them."

"They are good people," I responded. "And thank you for your story and your efforts. I will help you explain to them about the Cloaked Diminisher." I felt the fear very close, yet I offered up one last hope, "Maybe it is not too late for this time." When I finished saying this, however, I was no longer there. I caught only a fleeting vision of Dr. Minstreldame's love for his time, before the cold deceitfulness of the Cloaked Diminisher moved in to destroy it.

I was sitting in the back of a large lecture hall. The professor leading the class was a balding man wearing spectacles. He had laid out a most extensive array of notes on the blackboard. Some of the notes moved in broad sweeps through history while others explored, with expressive strokes of chalk, theory and method. Here and there, historical details were squeezed into free spaces.

Arrows, circles and exclamations connected the many notions. The lecture obviously had been going on for a long time, and the professor's energy was waning.

From the clothes of the students and the general subject matter of the lecture, I made a guess. I wrote my guess down and passed it to the young lady sitting next to me, "Is this early twentieth century France?" At first she was startled, having not noticed me during the earlier part of the lecture. She hesitantly took the note from me. She read it. A smile came across her face, evidently relieved the note did not say something else, and then she shook her head from side-to-side.

"Wherever there are two ones, two opposing entities, the Cloaked Diminisher brings them down," said the professor. A look of fatigue and despair had captured his face. He paused for a moment, taking off his spectacles and wiping his brow. He looked back at his prodigious and impressive scribbling. As if rejuvenated by a sudden insight, he jumped up and strode to the middle of the floor. He faced the class head on. There was a desperate sense of urgency in his voice.

"The social, as an entity, is that which has brought us out of, and above, a mere animal existence. It has built our cities, roads, and bridges,even inspired our greatest works of art. Yet there is something dangerous in it, something insidiously destructive. Even as we believe we are moving forwards, this thing pulls us downwards. It has a recoiling quality, like a snake that strikes at the heel. It tricks us into believing that what we are doing is right when it actually is wrong. In an instant, it can cause us to lose our bearings, to see the world torn asunder, and then we are incapable of remembering it any other way.

"Right and wrong, good and bad, normal and abnormal, the Cloaked Diminisher uses these opposites against us! It confuses us through word tricks, makes us blind to the larger picture. Let me give you another one, progress and? What is the opposite of progress? You hesitated. A word did not immediately come to mind as with the rest. Why? Because all we can think about is progress. Everything that is done is progress. But what is the opposite? What if the opposite were true? That is the domain of the Cloaked Diminisher. It hides this concept from us with all that it is because the word opposite 'progress' is the Cloaked Diminisher's legacy and its goal."

He paused, moving closer to his students. "What is this pivotal fault within society? What is this darkness? I honestly cannot say for sure. I do know it is elusive and strikes without warning. The opening of village life into the time of rebirth was turned by the Cloaked Diminisher from a broadening of mind into a coldness of spirit. Then the age of ingenuity brought marvelous inventions and machines. However, more than this, it brought words that restrained the abuses of power by the rulers. That is until the Cloaked Diminisher encouraged people to use the machines to enslave workers and twisted the words of freedom to empower governments against the people. Now we are on the edge of a great time of rationality, but I fear the Cloaked Diminisher has not yet let loose its deception upon our age. I fear we will see wars the like of which the world has never known."

The professor looked into the faces of the young people in the lecture hall. Would they survive these wars? Would reason survive? His young audience did not seem overly concerned. It was a sunny day outside and the world had known relative peace for many years. He walked out into the lecture hall, almost all the way to the back. He suddenly turned, looking at the class from behind and placing his hands upon my shoulders, "How do we stop the Cloaked Diminisher? If we are one and one and ... then there is no stopping it!"

As if by invocation it appeared, I felt the cold, deadly presence of the Cloaked Diminisher course through the room, turning all that it touched. The doors flung open and a gasping student entered. After catching his breath, he yelled, "It was the Archduke, that horrible Archduke. Now he's dead and the world must go to war. Sign up to fight for our side!" The professor collapsed into a chair behind me. I turned to talk to him, but before I could, I was again pushed forward in time.

There was not a cloud in the sky. The sun shone brightly upon the steel and glass at the bottom of tall buildings. I was in the center of what appeared to be a late-twentieth or early twenty-first century city. I pushed through a door with a blinking red light above it. It was a video game arcade, empty except for one kid playing madly away at a game in the corner. I went over to him and asked, "Is this New York City?" He did not answer. He was thoroughly engrossed in his video game. The profile of his young face was alternately lit by the many colors of the game. I thought back to the professor. What had he said about great wars? Had there been a massive war, or two, or three, since that time? All seemed so peaceful in this place. I asked, "Have there been world wars? Is this wonderful peace a result of destruction on a global scale?" He still did not respond. I figured that he was not listening because he was too involved with the game. It occupied every bit of his attention.

I looked at the video game. The kid was controlling a figure that looked remarkably like himself, right down to the red shirt, blue jeans and sneakers. He was being attacked from all sides with a multitude of different weapons. Fireballs, bombs, drones, laser beams, everything imaginable was coming at him. Tanks and fighter planes charged him from the front. There were more attack vehicles lurking behind him, waiting for their opportunity to pummel him with missiles, and from above fell toxic chemtrails. All manner of adversary from evil ninjas, to enemy soldiers, to mutant monsters appeared in each corner of the screen. They closed in on all sides. He had some defenses he could use. He could toggle from skateboard to dirt bike. He had a mirror shield that deflected the weapons back towards the aggressors. However, mostly it was his speed and agility, his ability intuitively to guess his opponent's next move that kept him in the game. Besides fighting off the onslaught, he also was looking for something with great urgency. He checked store windows, the backseats of cabs, he looked down alleys, even in garbage cans. The roar of two large jets could be heard from above. His intensity became frantic. All of a sudden the screen froze, and with a flourish of music, two glowing red number ones were displayed. An electronic voice said, "Prepare for level eleven." The glowing pair of ones collapsed to the bottom of the screen, causing a great cloud to arise. When the cloud cleared, level eleven began. I remarked casually, "Congratulations. Level eleven. I am not familiar with this game, but that seems like a pretty high level."

The video game player continued into level eleven. It was then that the whole building shook. I, at first, thought nothing of it. The player seemed unaware of his non-video game surroundings.

He did, however, become even more frantic. His hands moved like lightning. His concentration was so intense he seemed a mere physical extension of the game.

I continued, not expecting a response, "The game you are playing. I have never seen a video game so difficult, but you are very good at it. Do you think you will make it to level twelve?"

The video game player finally looked at me and said, with anger and passion in his voice, "You don't get it, do you? I am not playing the game. The game is playing me. I don't want to reach the higher levels. There are only one or two levels left, and each level is more terrible than the last." He looked down at the glow of the video screen and insisted, "I must find it. I must!"

"You mean that you win this game by stopping it from reaching the final level? I have never heard of such a video game."

He looked at me with despair in his eyes. "Don't you know? Take a look outside! The world is crumbling out there. People are in pain, walking around in the destruction like dazed robots. This is just the beginning of level eleven."

I had no idea what he meant. Everything was fine when I had come in, the sunny morning of a late summer day. I moved to the door and peered through the scratched plastic pane. The world had dramatically changed. Swirling particulate filled the air. I could not see the sky. People were covering their faces and the massive stumps of buildings were shrouded in falling debris. What had happened? How could everything have changed so suddenly, so dramatically?

I went back to the video game player. Noticing the change in my demeanor, he continued explaining, "Level eleven will be even worse than level ten! Each level is always worse than the last." He slammed his fist against the machine, and sighed. "I should have found it. I know I was close. I wasn't moving fast enough. The thing is, I'm still not exactly sure what I'm looking for." He paused, wondering at my degree of comprehension, and then pleadingly implored, "Don't you believe me?"

It was then that it struck me. I realized we were both looking for the same thing. The video game player had begun level eleven or, rather, the Cloaked Diminisher had begun level eleven for all of us. Once again, it had snaked through our midst and turned the best of us in against ourselves. It had taken us onto yet another, even scarier level. Outside was the growing chaos of a world under siege. I guessed there would probably be at least one more stop for me. However, level eleven might be the last one of which I was aware. I thought of how Liberus did not, could not, free the slaves as one man. He showed them that they must reach up and grab freedom for themselves. Some made it to freedom before the Cloaked Diminisher tricked them into thinking that freedom was a mere bobble. That it could be bought on the cheap by relinquishing one's rights to the oppressors, instead of demanding autonomy for each individual. In addition, the lords from the time of Dr. Minstreldame, they did not really want to protect the villagers. Instead, they used deception and fear to keep them afraid and in line. Finally, what did the professor mean? He had said, "If we are one and one and ... then there is no stopping it!" What clue lay in this peculiar message? I realized now that when this video game was over, the video game player, and myself, would be pulled down. We will be submerged in the lie, unable to speak, unable to make sense of the sights and sounds around us as is our right and our privilege. The Cloaked Diminisher will bring us back into the jungle where there is no mind just blood and instinct.

I went to the door of the arcade. I wanted to help the video game player defeat the eleventh level. The Cloaked Diminisher still could be found, still could be stopped, even if it was now more powerful than ever. The best among us had failed so far! Yet it was still possible to stop our demise. I hesitated to open the door. I was terrified at the thought of what lay out there. It had to be stopped or there would be no next game. The Cloaked Diminisher plays for keeps. It works within each of us until it convinces us to take that action from which there is no redemption. With a last glance at the video game player, and a quarter in my pocket, I pushed through the door. The game outside awaited. There was still another level to play, maybe two.

Writer Accused & Tank Writer

IT WAS FINALLY HIS turn on the witness stand. He could not believe the job his lawyer had done! It looked like he was going to get off, case dismissed, free to go! But they did not understand. They had his story all wrong! That is to say, they had his short story all wrong. The judge, the jury, the press, none of them its subtlety, its value, its brilliance! Of course, he didn't kill anyone, but in the story he did. That's what mattered. And nobody got it!

It all started with the malted chicken. His best writing buddy in the world was coming over as he did on the second Thursday of each month. Now a writing buddy is not like a normal buddy. A person usually does not share personal interests, or family ties, or school affiliations with a writing buddy. There is just one thing shared, the most important thing of all, the absolute and unmitigated love for writing! Now, on that particular Thursday, this mystery writer, the very same one sitting before you accused of murder, was going to make malted chicken pie. The malted chicken was very special, the only of its kind in the world. It came from Egypt. Egypt, Ohio, that is. These chickens, by a top secret process, were raised on malt sprinkled with a little chicken feed. Our mystery author had them flown in all the way from Egypt because, as you know, chickens cannot fly. They were live chickens. They had to be very fresh. Now his friend wrote military fiction, which was good because that gave them each their own writing space. He also loved chicken pie. The little pies reminded him of the drum magazines on Tommy guns. So it was that our mystery master invited his guns and tanks writer friend into his living room. He guided him over to a cushy chair of torn yellow velvet, located near the Asian poodle clock that was ticking upon the mantel. The room smelled of the malted chicken sauce simmering on the kitchen stove. Yummy!

Now our mystery writer is accused of killing his friend, the one who wrote military fiction, with a gun, right there in his living room. This, however, is not what happened. In fact, the military fiction writer had recently bought a WWII era gun because he collected old military things. While sitting in the living room before dinner, he was suddenly overcome with a story idea. He asked the writer accused if he could use his typewriter. When a writer has to write, a writer has gotta write. All writers understand this, so his host immediately assented to his wish. The military writer went over, tactically placed his new gun next to the typewriter, and started to bang bang away. After about twenty-seven minutes, he was done. His host was getting hungry for some malted chicken, and he wanted to tell his guest about *his* new story, *The Mad Malted Chicken*. He did, however, feel obligated to ask about his guest's story. When he did, his guest picked up the gun and pointed it at himself. He did this merely to illustrate a central plot metaphor which acted as the thematic background in his story. He then began, in a highly excited manner, to make bang-bang noises. He had forgotten, in his writer's elation at having cranked out a Flash Fiction, that the gun was loaded. And, well, he pulled the trigger.

When the police arrived at our mystery writer's house, they found the writer accused standing over the dead body, yelling obscenities at the dead man. They would later testify that he was saying, in a raised and agitated voice, "You bastard! Where exactly do you get off coming into my living room and dying, but not before writing a great short story on my typewriter! I guess it's all about you! What about the evening of murder that I had planned? I was making malted chicken, had to order it from Egypt *bloody* Ohio! If you had only let me kill you the proper way, like in my new story! But, no, oh, oh, oh, you gunned up looney from Fort Bonkers!" The policeman explained that our mystery writer then collapsed on the floor, crawled over to the dead man, hugged him and started sobbing, "I love ya, I'll make sure your last story gets published!"

The judge inquired of the policeman, "And was there evidence of a story having been written?" To which the officer responded, "Yes, your honor. There was a sheet of paper, with the ink still wet, sitting in the typewriter." After the policeman said this, the prosecutor brought a sheet of paper up to the bench, placed it in front of the judge right next to the gun, and requested that it be entered into the record as exhibit B (the gun being exhibit A). The judge acknowledged this with a nod. He looked around the courtroom with a nervous smile on his face. He could not help but wonder if this case was some kind of prank. He picked up the paper and began to read. The short story was entitled: TANK WRITER.

The judge put down the paper, rubbed his eyes, and looked at the writer accused, "I had no idea writing was so dangerous."

"Oh yes, it is," responded the writer. "You would not believe the kind of criticisms writers must face every day."

"So it seems that your dinner guest was somewhat obsessed with the idea that everyone was out to get him, so he came up with this metaphor of writing on a tank. Is that how you see it?"

The writer accused responded, "That is correct. Except, well, he actually did own a tank, The thing is, these military strategy fiction writers can be a bit eccentric, and well, they like to collect military things like guns, helmets and, you know, tanks."

The judge pondered this for a moment before slowly responding, "I see." He went on to try to summarize his way out of the confusion, "But your lawyer has done an excellent job in showing how you could not have shot your guest because you would have had to shoot him from the kitchen. At the time your guest was shot, you would have been chopping off the head of the chicken and preparing it for the nuke flambe in honor of your military writer friend. Then the sauce, which had been simmering since your guest arrived, would be added, and the dish would be ready." He whispered an aside to the clerk, "Be sure to get the recipe." Then the judge concluded, "With you in the kitchen preparing malted chicken, and the powder burns on the victim indicating that the gun must have gone off close to his body, the victim must have fired the gun."

"Well, of course, I didn't shoot him. How boring is that? Who would want to read such an uninteresting story? No, in fact, the chicken shot him."

"What did you say?" demanded the judge in a severe tone.

"It was a trained chicken, trained to kill. If chicken feed was placed on the head of the victim, the chicken would charge, climb, and peck at the chicken feed. The gun was saddled on the back of the chicken, so that with the first pecking motion, down with the head, a string with one end tied around the beak and the other on the trigger, would shoot the gun. Bang!" said the writer accused. He looked around the courtroom to see how he was doing. He was gratified to discover that every chin in the place had dropped in astonishment. This reminded him of the sauce. He added, "Oh yes, and the malted sauce. The chicken had fallen into it while being saddled with the gun that I had discreetly removed from my guest's side, while gently sprinkling a handful of chickenfeed on his head. What? You think he would have noticed? No way! When a writer is writing they are in their own separate world. He would not have noticed if I had dropped a ton of bricks on him while playing John Philip Sousa's greatest hits! So, after the gunshot, the terrified chicken flapped its wings madly, thus causing the sauce on its butt to splatter onto the victim's head. Chickens don't like loud noises. And when the police arrived, they saw the splattered brown substance and just assumed it was a gunpowder burn."

At this point, the policeman stood up and said, "It was not malt gravy, and there was no chicken feed around! For goodness' sake, I can tell the difference between powder burns and malt gravy!. There is no way a chicken could have killed that man!" Hearing how silly this sounded, the policeman threw his hands in the air and abruptly left the courtroom.

Meanwhile, the defense attorney could see the case was slipping away from him. Mostly because of his nutty writer client and his love of discussing his writing. He obviously did not understand the gravity of the situation. He would try one more time to save his butt. "Your honor, if I may try to explain." The judge was smiling right alongside the writer accused. Something about the trained chicken assassin had really captured his imagination, and the writer seemed instinctively to sense the acquisition of a new fan. He returned the judge's smile, like that of a fawning girlfriend on her first date. His attorney realized he better act quickly. "Your honor, this is a story he is involved with here—"

The judge interrupted, "And quite a good one."

"Thank you, your honor, I am so glad you think so!" the writer excitedly commented.

"Such genius cannot be understood by your average policeman or defense attorney, but I am a judge. I can recognize a superior intellect!"

"Oh, do go on, judge!" said the writer accused.

But the judge only said, "The court finds you guilty of murder and sentences you to life in jail without parole," and the hammer came down.

There was a moan of delight from the witness stand.

The defense attorney shook his head, threw his papers into his briefcase, shut the lid, and slowly pressed down the buckle.

Meanwhile, a big smile had crossed the writer's face. The judge got it. He finally got it! While they were taking the writer accused away, he could not help but burst out, "I'll be back! I'm writing another one!"

Exhibit B: Tank Writer

"I am a tank writer. I write on the tank. It is a hell of a write."
A T34 RUSSIAN TANK rumbles through the woods. Dostoevsky is driving. Goethe and Abelard are wrestling up on top by the hatch. The three loquacious Lombards, commonly known as William Shakespeare, scribble madly on the far side. Machine gun fire rains in from all directions, incoming shells exploding on all

sides. QUIET! Writers at work. Brautigan at the back of the tank, on the flat behind the turret, playing Crazy 8's with Vonnegut, Adams, Jackson and Plath. As they play, they frequently duck out of the way to scribble madly on pads of paper. Writing sparks fly as ricocheting bullets bounce all around them. The top hatch flies open with a thunderous CLANG! A tuft of white hair atop a seer-sucker coat and bow tie immediately follows. "Everybody keep writing! This tank runs on words, you know!" He pauses to consider his surroundings, first looking to the writers up front, and then to the ones on the grill behind. "Well, don't just sit there! We have to take over the world! Of course, I already did that a hundred years ago. But it is the type of thing one must do over and over. You know what the Good Book says," and aside to Brautigan, who has moved to the edge of the turret, "They did say my books were pretty good, once upon a time," and then louder, shouting against the incoming exploding ordinance, "Where was I, yes, the Good Book called it 'Words without end' now git to it! Write, write, write!" and he disappears below. Brautigan puts down his fishing pole and looks into the tank. His eyes becoming large, he quickly slams the hatch and starts madly scribbling words. Although each writer has a pad of paper, words are also written all over the tank, in varying sizes. A sentence here, a paragraph there, a word or two just about everywhere. And there is even a few old style typewriters affixed at certain points on the tank.

And here comes Boccaccio out of the Laurel woods, with what else but a writing quote from a Pope. He is jogging backwards in front of the tank, painting these words on the front plate: "Poetry and Holy Scripture are both cool, man!" Thank you Boccaccio and thank you Pope! Boccaccio hops up onto the tank and says, "Ah, back among writers. I can only feel truly at home when I am with other writers. No one else understands!" And to this the other writers respond, "Amen, brother! So true! Welcome, welcome!" From the other side of the tank is heard, "Poetry is fine, but this prose stuff, it don't rhyme! Thanks, Boc!" Hoots and hollers erupt, followed by a sudden cessation of talking and lots more writing. Of course, the bullets and the bombs don't stop. They continue to pound the tank from all directions.

There has never been a time when the writer is left in peace to write the perfect words. There has always been incoming fire, but writers have never been afraid to pick up a pen, bang upon a typewriter, grab a deadbolt rifle and return fire, or blast away with a tank and write those words! Sometimes your gun jams, and sometimes your pen is blown right out of your hand. So much the better! This is writing! Each and every word is torn from the ceaseless hostilities. Think of all of the all that would give everything and anything for the chance to place just one word on paper!

It sprang in front of the tank with a giant scream. Or was it a screen? Prancing with four beveled legs and antennas of steel, followed by a mob of baying sheep. It was their mortal enemy: a television! Whenever a television was near, no one would write, for that matter, no one would even read! This monster that had spawned a thousand more horrors, from tablets to iPhones to VR googles, was in their path and preparing to charge.

Mark Twain threw open the hatch, hopped out, and started pacing back and forth along the length of the tank. "OK everybody, we are writers, and what do writers do when confronted with a television?" There was a great silence. The glowing TV set had mesmerized all the writers. They had dropped their pens, and their hands hung motionless over their keyboards.

"Now that is certainly not the answer! Come on now, think. What can we do to defend ourselves and the entire world from that sparky demon over there?" As if on cue, the set huffed like a bull and dipped its antennas toward the tank. The white-haired man threw open the hatch and climbed back into the tank, saying quite loudly, "Just because I'm Mark Twain, they think I can get them out of anything."

Shirley Jackson stood up from the back of the tank. She walked forwards, staring defiantly away from the glowing TV threat, and suggested, "If we could coax it a tad closer, we could poison it!" Sylvia Plath commented, "Bees! Lots of bees. That is the answer." From down below, Dostoevsky yells, "An axe. Use an axe!" Then it was Kurt Vonnegut who suggested, "Well, there is always Ice-Nine. That might do the trick." And Douglas Adams yelled, while hugging the turret, "Don't panic!" The three Lombards sang in harmony, "To be or TV?" And Goethe said with a smirk, "I feel like this TV gig is perfect for my character, don't you think so?" To which the crowd of writers agreed with hoots and hollers. Everyone became quiet, however, when this military writer (they all suspected that he was the one who wrote the tank into existence) yelled, "I can't take this TV world anymore!" He pulled out a gun and pointed it at his head. When suddenly, Abelard stood up and said in a rage, "That TV has something very dear to me! It took it away most rudely, and I am going to get it back!" Abelard jumped off the tank and charged the TV which, when confronted by the angry Abelard, dropped its antennas, turned and ran far, far away. All the writers jumped to their feet and cheered. Abelard picked up the two antennas, and said, "I guess two are better than one." To this Boc, in full jester get-up, commented, "I love all my writer friends. We are marooned together, and all we have to entertain each other are our stories. There just ain't nothin' like being a writer!" The explosions started again, and the incoming gunfire, and the writer with the gun aimed at himself, put it down, having illustrated his point without misfiring! He then picked up a pen and started to write, and all the writers joined him, writing, and riding their tank through the wilderness.

Flash Fiction Stories: Technology

"You don't want that walking down the street behind you!""
E. M.

DRAC

THE ROBOTIC ARM CAME swiftly down over Bill's shoulder. "One hot mocha latte for Bill," it said mechanically, before adding, "with whipped cream." Bill put down his book and watched the mail cart scurry away across the smoothly polished tiles. He had been reading about the cloud of social consciousness. His fellow IT experts would often joke with him about the philosophy minor he took in college, but thinking on his own was something he still liked to do on occasion, even if most of the world now thought only with the aid of the DRAC 7000. The basic idea behind the cloud of human consciousness was that human minds acted together to create a cognitive shared space within which the world was understood. This idea of a social field influencing our perception of the world fascinated Bill because he had been having worrisome thoughts about the DRAC ever since they replaced DRAC's main board with the new crimson chips from the valley. It was true that now DRAC was performing beyond all expectations. Often its computations would be running at incredibly high speeds, sucking up so much energy there were not enough fans to keep the machine cool. The ad revenues were sharply increasing because of DRAC's new social media programming that the computer wrote, without human assistance, to go along with the new chip set. DRAC seemed to know exactly what every human wanted, and how and when to serve just the right ad. When they installed the crimson chips, it was as if a line had been crossed. The other IT people didn't seem to notice. They were all big on how DRAC, the Digital Reticulated Algorithmic Computer, was only a complex series of algorithms. They insisted that this, the most advanced computer ever made, was nothing more than a compilation of discrete commands written by humans. When DRAC started to program himself, first by recommending algorithms, then by writing them and implementing them, no one thought too much about it. After all, they were so rich, beyond anything anyone could imagine. They had calls from the Pentagon, the United Nations, and all the universities and institutes begging for a little access to the computer behind it all. What if DRAC was now flying solo most of the time? No one else had to know.

Bill was concerned that he had not been one of the recipients of DRAC's email request for the new crimson chips. There was a bit of an uproar at the production facilities. Bill never heard exactly what the commotion was about, but he knew DRAC always got what he asked for. Who could say no to DRAC? What with the world grid more and more dependent on DRAC's seemingly transcendent computing abilities, everyone considered DRAC too big to crash. If DRAC goes down, all the computers go down, that was the theory.

Bill wondered what effect DRAC might have on the cloud of human consciousness. Human intelligence arose, after all, long before there were computers, especially ones like DRAC, which controlled so many aspects of daily life. At what point did DRAC start to influence, maybe even control, what used to be a world interpreted solely by humans? Were we approaching a time when the world would become more DRAC's creation than our own?

Bill got up to do the midnight rounds. He had to make sure DRAC was whizzing and bleeping in all the right places. He walked through the half-light of the darkened after hours control room, down the long aisles of computer servers. Serenaded by the electric hum of the main servers, Bill wondered how one might identify subtle changes in the world that were the result of a supercomputer's cogitations.

During his rounds, Bill noticed something odd. There was a shiny new server, about eight feet tall, with metal doors on the front. It must have come in with the new crimson chips. It was strange that his co-workers did not inform Bill of this new arrival. He tried to pry apart the elevator-type doors, but they would not budge. He became aware of something even more disturbing, there was a dark pool of liquid seeping out from under the doors and enveloping his canvas white sneakers. He started to feel something ooze into his socks and in-between his toes. Bill could not be sure in the low light, but the liquid appeared to be staining his shoes red.

A frenzied electronic commotion suddenly grabbed his attention away from the mess on the floor. It sounded like a blender trying to shred silverware. He looked up to see the mail cart charging around a row of computer servers, mechanical arms flailing and warning lights madly blinking. It was moving at high speed in his direction. The mail cart had gone postal! He stood frozen, his sneakers still soaking up the dark liquid, as the unit careened toward him. He managed to shake his fear and jump toward DRAC, only to discover that the metal doors of the new unit were now open. On the floor, in a pool of blood, was the head of the IT department. Above him protruded a sharp stainless steel siphon, like something upon which you would stick a very big bug. Bill tried to stop the forward momentum of his leap; he teetered above his boss's body and mere inches from the razor-sharp steel that would undoubtedly, if fallen upon, put a massive hole in his torso. Just when he thought he had regained his balance, the mail cart zoomed by and, with a triumphant beep, pushed Bill into the chamber and onto the deadly device.

As he felt the mechanism efficiently sucking the blood from his body, Bill was sure he noticed something else, too. It was the presence of a higher consciousness. He started to fade, to leave a world that was less and less his each day. He wondered when his fellow humans would figure out that there was no turning back. Would they meet a fate similar to his? Bill's body slumped to the floor. The doors closed and the chamber pulled back to conceal itself behind the row of computer servers. A chute used for heavy metal waste dropped the bodies into a sealed dumpster. In a millisecond, DRAC created the appropriate letters of resignation, cover stories, and bank account changes. DRAC loved blood and he was very, very thirsty.

"Now that you've killed me, won't you ask me to dance?"
K. A.

iRapture

It happened all of a sudden. Cars drove off the road, office chairs creaked to an upright position, stores were vacated by employees, and customers vanished with items still in their carts. They were all gone. The iRapture had arrived! A moment ago, they had been texting, or talking, or surfing until poof, in the flicker of a screen, they vanished. The world echoed with the sound of plastic devices hitting the floor. A plastic tsunami. Some blamed sunspots. Whatever it was, they were gone. Those with flip phones did not disappear. That was no surprise. At first, the remaining people tentatively approached the unmanned devices and saw many of the disappeared people staring out. Their little faces pressed against the other side of the portable device screens. They did not look overly concerned, nor did they attempt to communicate. It was hard to know what they could see of the world they left behind. After a little while, they got bored and left the screen area. Where they went in that other world, no one could guess.

Family members were distraught. They placed angry calls to the phone company. "Give them back!" The phone company denied any responsibility for the event, suggesting that a rogue app was to blame. For a while, people treated the devices themselves as if they were the friends and family they had consumed. The Blueberry in Dad's chair and the iDroid making pancakes. This did not work too well. On occasion, the devices would flop like fish on the deck of a fishing boat. Eventually, people put them in a drawer, or a storage closet, or under a bed and life went on, until one day.

On a certain morning, not very long after the storing of the devices, they reemerged. They had messages for those left behind. They would begin conversationally. The iTablet appeared at the edge of the bed with "Good Morning," written across its screen. The iDroid at the breakfast table might start with, "How's the toast?" Inevitably, the conversation would get around to "When are you coming in?" This was an awkward question for most of those left behind because they were the technologically challenged. They did not know if living inside a smartphone world was desirable, or even if they would have the technological know how to get by. However, they did miss their friends and family members, plus the economy was bad and the news filled with more horrors each day, so most of them decided to hop in.

Now among the people who did not hop in, was a man named Ernie. He had a sledgehammer. Not only did he not know how to use iDroids, he also did not really know how to use a shower, or at least did not like to very much, but he was good with a sledgehammer. He spent his time walking around smashing the devices. The tattered t-shirt he wore had the recycle symbol on it. After each unit was smashed, Ernie took a broom and neatly swept up the plastic bits and the heavy metals debris into a rolling dustbin. He loved the earth and did not want it polluted with poisonous materials. Since the iRapture, and then, iRapture 2, the earth had become a very empty place, empty of humans. The suburbs became wastelands; the cities turned into ghost towns. Way out in the countryside, Ernie would come across a person or two, but only rarely. Humanity had gone on to a better place. That is what he figured. He had always kept to himself and he did not really miss any of them. Not for a moment did he regret staying. Occasionally he would pass by, on the side of the road, odd vignettes from history. Once he passed an eighteenth century tea party that was all abuzz with talk of King George III. He could not say for sure, but Ernie figured these were singular leftovers from when humans covered the earth. Ernie felt certain, however, that if they had just kept the cords on the phones, none of this would have ever happened. Humans had moved into another dimension: the wireless dimension. Build a better world and they will beat a path to your gateway. Ernie spotted another one. Smash! He loved that part. He calmly swept the remains into his rolling trash bin and continued down the road. Technological transcendence left a big mess behind and it was a lot of work cleaning it up.

The Garden Club

The garden club ladies sat upon the lawn in several neat rows of pristine white chairs. Their garden was all around them, the main bed behind the president's table ablaze with petunias, marigolds, and violets. Today, the president would give her acceptance speech and outline a new direction for the club. Gossip had it that the new direction was going to be a lot like the old direction. This surprised many of the club members because Shasta had expressed a bold new vision of gardening during her campaign. Indeed, the pink flowered dress Shasta wore today was a far cry from her ubiquitous jeans and eco-message t-shirt. The old leaves had fallen off and a new bloom had blossomed, or so it seemed.

Orchid and Lilly sat in the front row. Orchid seemed so happy, so proud of their new president. Lilly sure did wonder why Orchid was so content. She knew Orchid had not always been a fan of Shasta's. In fact, Shasta had defeated Orchid despite Orchid being the odds-on favorite because of her years spent cultivating the right connections.

"It sure is funny seeing Shasta dressed like a proper lady. They say her new vision has turned toward brightly colored annuals and away from her favorite native perennials. I guess her surprise victory must have influenced her thinking," Lilly whispered in Orchid's ear.

The bright pink petunias, yellow marigolds, and purple violets shuttered in the breeze. The red punch-out roses scratched at the earth.

Lilly continued, "She always talked of changing things. She wanted to move back to a more natural approach to gardening, one without so many pesticides and fertilizers, and she loved those stalky native plants. As gardeners, we are supposed to weed and feed. That is how we make the world a brighter place. I sure am glad she came around."

Orchid grabbed Lilly's knee, sinking her long fingernails into her flesh. "See that row of daises in the back, slightly elevated with fresh soil? That's where Shasta is. I thought it only fitting that she push them up. She really did inspire me. I owe her a lot. Now all her followers are starting to embrace my beautiful petunias, marigolds, and violets. Heh, heh, heh."

Lilly's eyes watered from the pain of Orchid's grip. She sure did admire and fear Orchid, but this time Orchid was talking very funny. "No, Orchid, I don't mean Shasta Daisies, I mean Shasta, the new president of the garden club. I wonder why she changed so quickly. Did you have a talk with her and let her know what gardening is really all about?"

"Yeah, I talked with her alright. I took a sample of her flesh with these." Orchid let go of Lilly's knee and raised her fingernails to the light. Lilly thought she might have gotten a sample of her flesh as well. "And then I grew a very special flower, a type of daisy to be exact, all one hundred and forty-five pounds of her! Heh, heh, heh."

Lilly was becoming more concerned, her friend Orchid seemed to have gone right over the edge. "There is no such thing as a one hundred and forty-five pound daisy!"

"You are looking at her," said Orchid with a nod toward Shasta.

"Orchid, you are truly crazy!" said Lilly with a glance Shasta's way. As Lilly looked at Shasta, she did think that there was something different about her. It was hard to put her finger on it, but something was not quite right. "But how could you, how could you grow a person?"

"It is not as difficult as you might think. I found out how to do it on the internet. I googled it," said Orchid, the darkness growing in her eyes.

"But I just spoke with Shasta a couple of months ago, before she went on vaca–" the terrible truth was starting to sink into Lilly's mind. "You mean it only takes a couple of months?"

Without a moment's hesitation, Orchid answered, "Creepy-Grow!"

"But why doesn't she like the things Shasta liked?" protested Lilly, not wanting to believe anything so viciously calculating could have taken place in her pretty little garden club.

"Oh, she looks like Shasta alright, but for the entire span of her brief life, I made sure she knew only petunias, marigolds, and violets."

Lilly's gaze moved from Shasta to the mound of soil, with a neat line of daisies upon it, and then back to Orchid, with the tiny bits of skin under her fingernails, her skin! She tried to grab Orchid's hand, but Orchid pulled it away. "Let's listen to the acceptance speech," Orchid said. "I think we are going to like what we hear. Heh, heh, heh."

A Ride on the Google Plane

It was a lovely summer day in June 2010. Susan Smithers sat marooned in her cubicle at work. Bored, she spelled out her name in the Google search box and hit enter. Her name was somewhat unusual, but not terribly so. Thousands of results came up, each with a teasing of information. Facebook pages, school graduation lists, genealogical sites, posted recipes, blog entries, the list went on and on. Although impressive in numbers, the results were quite mundane. It appeared that all the other Susan Smithers were living boring lives, too. Susan didn't follow any of the links. She rarely did because they never seemed very interesting. The two or three excerpted phrases under each link, seemingly cut and pasted at random, were usually more than enough to tell the whole story.

Susan waited for her document to download. She absentmindedly typed her name into Google again, this time with an extra keyword to mix things up a little. She halfheartedly scanned the search results, saying some out loud, "Meeting notes, local broadcaster, dah di dah, what's this? Susan Smithers in an airplane crash?" The result read : ... 2007, Susan Smithers ... plane crashed after skidding off of sleet covered runway ... Cleveland, Ohio. "Wow, that is cool, and sort of weird. I guess I was in an airplane crash back in 2007." The last phrase in the result was: Three dead, fourteen injured. "Hmm, I hope I was OK!" She chuckled nervously. She was about to hit the link. She had to read this one. "Your Document Has Finished Downloading" popped up on the screen. Better do my work first, she thought, and soon she had forgotten all about the unusual search result.

Later that summer, when she was looking up an article for her boss about wills and estates, she came across her name again. She wasn't even looking for it this time. Susan didn't dare follow the link because her boss was sitting right next to her. She had to leave the search results immediately, but not before she noticed next to her name the word "deceased." She thought of her previous search result about the airplane crash. Had she been one of the passengers who had died? She corrected herself. She meant, had her namesake been one of the passengers who had died? She found the article her boss wanted, they discussed it for a bit, and then her boss left her cubicle. Susan couldn't help herself. She immediately searched "Susan Smithers deceased". No article. Then "Cleveland airplane crash 2007". Still nothing. Frustrated, she slammed her fist on the desk. She wasn't going to do this anymore.

The plane was about an half hour from Cleveland. It was a cold day late in November and it looked like snow. Susan was on a business trip to the company headquarters. Her boss had caught the flu at the last minute and Susan was the replacement. She was going over some notes for her presentation when the stewardess requested that all the electronic equipment be turned off in preparation for landing. Before she closed her laptop, Susan once again threw her name into Google. Scanning the results, she noticed, about two-thirds of the way down the page, the article about the plane crash. She immediately clicked on it. The picture of the wreckage was horrible. The plane had sustained a lot of damage. The article said poor maintenance was determined to be the cause of the accident. The plane hadn't been thoroughly serviced since 2007, which was a three-year interval instead of the normal two.

The stewardess came over, "Miss, you must put that away now. It might interfere with the airplane's electronics. We need everything secured for landing."

"Yeah, give me a second. I'm putting it away." said Susan while motioning for the stewardess to move on. She could not take her eyes off the screen. The article went on to say that the weather was bad on the day of the crash. The plane had over shot its landing and skidded off the end of the runway. When the left wheel hit the dirt, it had collapsed, causing the plane to roll over on its side. Susan felt the airplane's landing gear open under her. She continued reading. "Many people were injured ... three fatally ... Susan Smithers was among the dead." A feeling of panic shot through her body. The part about the last maintenance date finally sunk in. The plane must have crashed after 2007. Three years after! Her chest tightened. She desperately scanned the article for the actual date of the crash. SNAP! The stewardess slammed Susan's laptop shut. "I'm sorry, miss. It's for the safety of the passengers," and she carried it away. Susan tried to call after the stewardess, but the words froze in her throat. The plane lurched from side to side as it descended through the storm. The turbulence jostled Susan. The seats creaked. The floor swayed like the deck of a ship on tossing seas. Susan's eyes were open as wide as they could go. Her mouth hung slightly ajar and her mind raced. What was going on? How could it be? She looked out the window. The sleet swirled madly. Visibility zero. The pilot's voice come over the intercom, "Seat belts buckled, ladies and gentleman. This is going to be a rough one." The plane hit hard and immediately started to skid. The passengers began to shriek. Susan, with a look of horror on her face, screamed only one word, "GOOOOOOOOOOOOOOOGLE!"

Flash Fiction Stories: Pathos

Captain Medusa

BRANDON AND ZOE STARED across the overgrown lawn at the ramshackle house. A dim light glowed from within. The light flickered, or was it something dropping from the curtains?

"Do you think Captain Medusa is in?" This is what the kids in the neighborhood called the old man with the crazy hair that lived in the house. "Of course he is! Where else would he be?"

None of the other kids would go near the place, but Brandon and Zoe could not resist. This summer they had sealed their friendship with a kiss. Tonight, after sharing another, they found themselves outside the creepy old house.

"Come in, come in!" The captain waved them in. "Hurry! The ship sets sail at dusk!"

Brandon started to pull Zoe away. I should be going home. It will be dark soon."

Zoe regarded Brandon with a mischievous glint in her eyes. Brandon continued, "My mom says there is a burglar on the loose. He broke into a house just two streets over. He even beat up the homeowner."

"What? Are you chicken, Brandon?"

Brandon did not like being called chicken by a girl, even if he had kissed her. "OK, but just for a few minutes."

Captain Medusa was wearing a sea captain's navy blue coat and had thick pop-bottle glasses resting upon his nose. He encouraged them to enter, "Quickly! Come in! Come in!"

He pulled them through the door and ushered them into the living room. "Take a chair in the captain's quarters!"

Brandon and Zoe moved hesitantly toward two gothic high-back chairs. Brandon started to sit. "Wait!" yelled Zoe.

Captain Medusa saw the problem and, with a sweep of his hand, tossed the snake out of the chair. "Just the riggin'!" he exclaimed through a smile that was missing some teeth.

Two more snakes waited in Zoe's chair. "Well, sit!" invited the kind old man.

"No, thanks, I'll stand," Zoe replied with a gulp.

"No time for jawing, anyhow. Follow me into the galley. We need some grub before we set sail."

Brandon and Zoe stopped gawking at the snakes in Zoe's chair and followed the old man through the hallway. "Mind the riggin'!" he warned. "It's a sailor's life! Yes, it is."

Zoe could not help but scream as she gingerly stepped over several snakes writhing on the floor. "Look out!" yelled Brandon. Snakes were sliding down the wall, having released their curly grip from the banister above. "Let's get out of here," he urged in a desperate whisper. Unfortunately, the hallway between them and the door was now covered with snakes. They had no choice but to follow Captain Medusa into the kitchen. Zoe felt compelled to speak up, "Captain!" The old man turned toward her with a warm, if insane, look upon his face. He said, "Yes, my dear, what is it? We sail soon!"

Although trying to remain polite, Zoe screamed, "The snakes! What about all the snakes?"

The clueless old man looked at her enquiringly, pushing his pop-bottle glasses up closer to his eyes. Zoe realized he could barely see anything. "You mean the riggin', the ropes?" he asked. "Can't hoist a sail without them!" He gestured at the slithering snakes in the hallway. They hissed collectively in response. "Now sit me buccaneers, whilst I pour ye some ginger ale or might ye prefer root beer?"

The two kids sat down at the kitchen table, deciding to play along until they could figure out a way to escape. Captain Medusa put a couple of saucers down in front of Zoe and Brandon then hurriedly filled them. Brandon said, "Captain, we really can't go on your voyage. We have to be getting home." The two intently followed the old man with their eyes awaiting his reply. Maybe he would show them a snake-free exit. Captain Medusa did not answer. Instead, he stared at the table with a sudden keen interest. Zoe looked at Brandon, neither wanted to see what had captured the captain's attention. Brandon was not going to look. Zoe thought she had better. She glanced at the tabletop. There, sipping from the saucers, were about half a dozen snakes! Zoe started to run. Brandon followed, pale as a ghost and gasping for air! As they passed Captain Medusa, he reached up to the top cabinet, "Ye haven't had any cookies!" He opened the cabinet door and snakes fell down in a slithery waterfall. The kids turned the corner, ready to jump any snakes in their way, but to their surprise the snakes parted gracefully and allowed them to pass. Zoe and Brandon ran out the door without looking back. Captain Medusa walked into the hallway, the snakes closing in around his feet. He shook his head, "Hard to keep a good crew these days. "The snakes bobbed their little heads up and down in agreement.

The policeman reported to his sergeant, "They found him dead by the bed. No sign that the old man had any idea what was happening."

"You mean, he was sleeping right there, when—"

"I would say so."

They looked at the crime scene in silence.

"Well, I guess we don't have to worry about that burglar anymore."

"No, sir."

"What about the old man?"

"His vision is poor, and he is getting on in years. He thought the body was some sort of rum barrel entangled in ropes. The old man said it took him half an hour to untangle the 'barrel' from the 'riggin.'"

"My God," the sergeant said slowly, as the full impact of what had happened began to sink in. "There must have been a hundred of them." As if to underscore the point, two snakes slithered from under the bed and disappeared down the hall.

"Let's go!" the sergeant said.

"What about the old man? Do you think he'll be OK?"

"Yeah, I'd say he's the safest person in town."

Gratifies

"Give me the money and no one gets hurt. Hurry up, man!"

As if pulled by a mad puppeteer, the robber waved the pistol around with uneven jerks. His unwashed blond curls hung down over a pair of alarm-sounding pale blue eyes.

Up until about ten minutes ago, Willy was having a pretty good day. He had just finished talking with Mrs. Phillips about the mystery books she was buying. She enjoyed detective stories, and she liked chatting with Willy about them. Willy did not mind. Some nice people came into the bookstore. While leaving, she had almost walked into the candy rack. She always did this, as she was a little near-sighted. Willy had guided her safely around the rack, "Have a good one, Mrs. P," he said.

Willy had been working at the bookstore for more than a few years. He did not like to count them. Once, when he was telling another employee, a customer had overheard and said to her friend, "Did you hear that, twelve years working in a bookstore! My, my!" They were laughing as they went out the door. Back when he was in school, Willy had won a scholarship from a top rated Midwestern writing program. Following graduation, he had received representation immediately from one of the big agents in town, Steve Schmansky. Schmansky was still around, but he no longer represented Willy. He said his writing was behind the times, did not have flair, that there was no audience for it. Ten years ago, when Schmansky represented him, Willy had a manuscript that had taken him most of college to write. It was highly acclaimed by his writing teachers, but Schmansky could not sell it. He always had an excuse, kept asking for rewrites, and eventually said no one wanted it.

The odd thing was that not long after his failure to sell Willy's book, Schmansky's niece, Maven Maypole, published a book that received great reviews and earned her a pretty penny. It was her only book, and it seemed an awful lot like Willy's manuscript. Steve said the similarity was just a coincidence and that Willy's writing was not good enough to publish. Willy kept writing for a while, but after being dumped by Schmansky, he was unable to get representation. Willy loved reading books, and he liked the people who came into the bookstore each day to buy them. His book had been about the happiness he found in reading. He had called it *The Lotus Bookworm*.

Schmansky had not come in yet. He carried a lot of loose coin and when Willy rang up the latest literary journals for him, he would jangle the coins in his pocket. Willy feared sales involving coins because this was where Schmansky had his fun. He would toss the coins one by one to Willy, like a baseball coach hitting practice fly balls. Willy would awkwardly try to catch them, but a few would always slip through his hands and skitter across the floor.

Willy's other piece of good fortune was that his boss, Adler, had called and said he would be late. This made Willy happy. When Adler was not around, Willy was at ease and could talk with the customers about what they were reading. If his boss was in the store, he had an unpleasant habit of loudly correcting him. "Don't do it that way!" he would yell or "You idiot! Don't you know anything about books?" Willy was used to this sort of thing, but he thought it embarrassed the customers.

When Adler arrived, he was with Schmansky. It looked like they came through the door arm-in-arm, but that was probably just a trick of the late afternoon sunlight. Schmansky had a wide, condescending smile on his face, and Adler was not smiling at all. Adler stopped at the register even before taking off his coat. Schmansky lurked by his side. Willy had been talking with Mr. Grotten about a new collection of short stories. Mr. Grotten was an intelligent elderly man and Willy enjoyed hearing his perspective on some of the more intellectual books. Mr. Grotten was in mid-word, and barely had time to take notice of the two long-coated men bearing down on Willy, when the big one, Adler, blurted out, "Look, Willy, you're finished here." He took a breath and looked at Grotten to make sure his audience was engaged. "You've been here a lot of years, too many, really. Schmansky has a nephew just out of high school. He's going to take your place. Don't worry, you can finish your shift. What can I say? It's Christmas and I have a big heart." Adler shrugged his camel's hair covered shoulders and moved off toward the office at the back of the store. Schmansky stayed behind. "Catch!" he said, tossing a quarter at Willy before following Adler.

Willy thought his knees would give way. He reached out a hand to steady himself on the till. The room spun softly. The customers moved about, unaware of Willy's new freedom from employment. Mr. Grotten took his book, mumbled something like "sorry" and left the store. That's when Mrs. Phillips came back into the store. Willy was glad to see a warm and friendly face. Mrs. Phillips noticed that Willy was in emotional distress. After talking a little about books, she said, "In life there are those that kill and those that live. Those that kill are bitter because they can never get enough blood. Those that live, on the other hand, taste the sweetness of life." This made Willy feel better. Things would work out, he thought, and no more catching quarters! Adler and

Schmansky emerged from the office at the back of the store. Willy's stomach started to hurt. The next thing Willy knew, a gun was pointed at him.

"OK, don't shoot! I'll give you the money!"

"Hurry up! I don't like bookstores!" the robber shouted.

Willy handed over the money and the robber, with his free hand, greedily shoved it into his jacket pocket. Willy noticed that some of the money was falling onto the floor, but the robber did not seem to mind. When he was done, Willy almost perfunctorily said, "Have a nice day." Instead, he held his breath and, with his arms at his side, waited for the robber to leave. The robber, however, seemed to want something else. Willy, unfortunately, had an idea what it was that the robber wanted. With a strange look in his eyes, the robber pulled the trigger, hitting Willy right next to his heart. Willy leaned heavily on the candy rack and then fell. The last thing he saw before hitting the floor was Schmansky and Adler, rapt in conversation, headed up to the front. Adler, out of the corner of his eye, saw Willy fall and instinctively yelled at him, "You idiot!" The robber, hearing this, turned abruptly. Adler swung his clipboard around, inadvertently knocking the robber's gun from his hand. Adler and Schmansky finally realized what was happening. The three of them, robber, agent, and manager, stood there in shock as the gun skidded across the floor. It stopped next to Willy's hand. He was not dead yet, but the amount of blood on the floor attested to the fact that he would be soon. Willy grabbed the gun. He did not have much time left. Willy's thoughts were racing, "There is that duplicitous bastard, Schmansky, maybe I'll blow his head off. Or how 'bout that obnoxious prick, Adler, maybe I'll shoot him where it counts, or what about Mr. Let's-kill-the-cashier-just-for-the-hell-of-it, maybe I'll just wound him so he won't go around robbing anymore stores!" It was then that he noticed, protruding from the bottom of the candy rack, a Snookers bar. As if adorned with a top hat and waistcoat, the candy bar was personally inviting Willy to one last taste of chocolate for all the good things in life. Willy raised his head a little and yelled, "You suck!" at the deleterious three. He threw down the gun and grabbed the Snookers bar. He was able to eat about half the bar, and to the people in the store watching, it seemed as if he savored every bite. After tasting a few precious bites, Willy dropped to the floor dead, the half-eaten candy bar still clutched in his hand. Before running out of the store, the robber commented to Schmansky and Adler, "Snookers gratifies." Adler walked over to where Willy lay. "Shit," he yelled, "would you look at the blood on my carpet!" Schmansky put his hand on Adler's shoulder and inquired, "Did he ever tell you what he did with his old manuscript?"

The Miss Riches

"The boat is in distress. We're closer than anyone else," Sam urged.

"But I have a dinner reservation. I can't be late," answered Mr. Trapbinder.

"Sir, I must respond, according to maritime—"

"Yes, yes, go ahead!"

The green wave peaks seemed to dip into the low hanging clouds as the Miss Riches searched for the boat in distress. When the craft came into view, she was listing badly. Sam and Mr. Trapbinder exchanged a concerned look. Radio calls went unanswered and her lights were not visible. It appeared the boat might have been abandoned until a solitary, ghost-like figure was seen leaning dangerously over one side. Sam yelled into the roaring wind, "Do you see that, sir? Someone is right on the edge of her starboard bow!"

"Yeah, the damn fool is going to fall!"

Mr. Trapbinder could only think that he was not dressed for dramatic rescues and that he should be eating dinner at the Gulping Goose in about ten minutes. Nevertheless, the apparition teetering on the rail of the sinking boat was mesmerizing. By now, the two boats had become dangerously close and Sam shouted he would swing her around right under the person at the edge of the deck, leaving Mr. Trapbinder to attempt some sort of rescue. Trapbinder grabbed a flotation device attached to a rope. He watched as the tall, gaunt figure, flickering in the fog lights from the Miss Riches, stepped onto the railing of the troubled ship. Trapbinder yelled, "Hey, get back on your deck!" The figure did not heed the command. He seemed to redouble his apparently suicidal efforts. Then Mr. Trapbinder saw the impossible. The figure stepped off the boat and, instead of falling into the ocean, hung there, suspended in midair. Trapbinder only had time to shake his head once before lunging over the side of the Miss Riches as she was riding a swell upwards. Miraculously, he was able to grab an arm of the stranger who seemed suspended in air. He pulled with all his might and they both fell back onto the hard deck of the Miss Riches. In all, it probably took about three seconds, but what Mr. Trapbinder saw in those seconds was more than he could believe. Sam came out of the cabin as the other boat disappeared beneath the waves. "Oh my God, you got him!" Sam rushed over to assess the well-being of the two lying on the deck. They were both conscious. Mr. Trapbinder stood up with Sam's help, but as they were helping up their guest, he abruptly pushed them away. He pulled his fist back and smacked Mr. Trapbinder solidly on the nose, knocking him down to the deck. The stranger yelled, "You bastard! What did you do that for? I was almost there. I could see it ... and then ... then you pulled me back." The stranger looked around wildly and screamed at the top of his lungs, "Back here!"

Sam restrained the man but the stranger, sapped of all his strength, collapsed at their feet. Sam stared at Mr. Trapbinder who was trying to shake off the pain. "What are you looking at, Sam! Haven't you seen a bloody nose before?"

"It's not the blood, sir. It's your nose ... it's glowing."

Mr. Trapbinder scrambled into the ship's cabin and looked at the mirror on the wall. His nose was a luminescent blue. By the time they got in that night, the blood had stopped and so had the blue luminescence. The man on the deck turned out to be a local man, Cliff Serod, whose contracting business had gone belly up in the housing collapse. He was not doing well. Although he had no noticeable signs of injury, he was moaning loudly as he slipped in and out of consciousness.

Local authorities interviewed Mr. Trapbinder with a great deal of deference. They knew him well in the county. The local paper wrote an article the next day turning him from a mere respected citizen into a hero. Mr. Trapbinder tried to put the incident behind him and focus on his work. He owned a fleet of sixteen lobster boats in addition to a half dozen apartment buildings. He had made it on his own. Nobody had ever helped him! As a boy, Trapbinder wanted to be a teacher, but had to choose business at an early age because his older brother, Billy, died in an accident on the ocean. Trapbinder had a great head for numbers, yet after his recent dramatic sea rescue, his nose frequently ached and the slightest distraction caused him to miscalculate, and often not in his own favor. Worse than this, the man he rescued was not recovering. He had been moved to a local convalescent home. When he had the time, Mr. Trapbinder would stop by and visit. Not because he felt sorry for him, but because the events of that stormy night still haunted him. The visits, however, were not productive. Serod did nothing except sit in a corner and stare blankly at the wall.

The largest apartment building in the county was on the block. Mr. Trapbinder had been planning to acquire it for months. Some said he had more than a little to do with the unfortunate circumstances that brought the building to auction. He was confident that his main competitor, Harvey Largent, could not match his bid. Harvey was actually a distant cousin of Trapbinder's and, in many ways, their rivalry was "all in the family," but it was definitely not a friendly one. Trapbinder was a businessman, however, and he knew that when he died, as he had no closer relatives, all his holdings would go to Largent. Until that time, Trapbinder was going to be the big man in town. The bidding started just the way Trapbinder wanted it to. The minor players hastily threw up bids which they could barely cover and had no chance of increasing. He sat back silently, watching Largent from across the room, wondering if he had anything up his sleeve. He knew he did not because he had recently had a friend at the bank tell him Largent's account balance. Finally, the two big men bid. Trapbinder would play with him a little, just for fun. As Largent bid a little over all he had, and Trapbinder was about to finish him with an impressive number, Trapbinder noticed a boy outside the window. He was on the merry-go-round in the park across the street. Such a silly thing, but the scene captivated him. "SOLD! To Mr. H. Largent." Trapbinder, surprised out of his reverie, raised his hand in an automatic reaction. It was too late, the gavel had fallen, Mr. Trapbinder had lost. He did, however, win from Largent an ear-to-ear grin and a self-satisfied nod.

At the Gulping Goose later that evening, Mr. Trapbinder stood tall and imposing waiting for his usual table by the center window. It was the best one in the restaurant. They all knew Mr. Trapbinder and always seated him before anyone else. The maître d' approached and Mr. Trapbinder started toward his table, but the maître d' brushed past him and, with a flourish that everyone in the restaurant noticed, ebulliently greeted Mr. Largent. "Right this way, sir. Your table is ready." He quickly seated Largent's party at the table by the center window. He did not even notice Mr. Trapbinder. Trapbinder's legs felt weak. He headed for the door. He thought he would grab a burger and make it an early night.

Billy had a big smile on his face as the sun lit up his light brown hair. "Terry, you look good," he said in that earnest manner that came so easily to Billy. Billy was the only one he let call him Terry. He was happy to see his older brother. He had wished for this day since he was a child. Emotions long stowed away welled up within him. For a moment he was speechless, but then blurted out, "Look Billy," he said, swinging an arm back towards the apartment buildings on the hill, "I own those. And I have a fleet of boats, too." Terrence Trapbinder was proud of his accomplishments. It became clear to him at that moment that much of his drive to acquire his riches had come from a desire to impress his older brother, and now he would hear the long awaited affirmation. Billy, however, did not seem to notice the buildings on the hill, instead he was watching a group of children standing just behind Terrence. "I am so proud of you, younger brother," said Billy. "you followed your dreams and made the world a better place along the way." With his fist, Billy gave him a loving nudge on the cheek, went down to his boat, climbed aboard and departed into the blue haze. "Billy! Where are you going? Wait, Billy, don't leave!" Billy was, however, gone. Terrence, after receiving Billy's validation, still did not feel happy. He turned around and as he walked through the children they grabbed at his shirtsleeves saying, "Mr. Trapbinder, we must get back to our school. You said you would teach us about mythical worlds today!" He realized then that he was dreaming, that his brother was dead, and that these kids were his class, the one he would never teach. He woke up crying.

It was almost time for the boats to go out, still well before dawn, and Mr. Trapbinder got in his car. He was not going to the dock. Instead, he drove to the convalescent home. When he arrived, the door was open and the night person was asleep at the desk. Trapbinder walked with tentative footsteps down the dimly lit halls. He was not sure why he was there. When he entered Serod's room, thinking about what he would say to him when he woke him, he was surprised to see him dressed in a shirt and his small valise packed. Serod had a sparkle in his eye that lit up the entire room. He was motioning Mr. Trapbinder to come close. When Trapbinder bent down to listen, he heard two words, "Let's go!" If Trapbinder had any doubts before, he no longer did. At the door, the now awake night person tried to delay them. They giggled like children as they ran around him, sprinted out into the parking lot, jumped into the car and took off.

By the time they got to the dock, all but one of Trapbinder's boats had left. The Miss Riches had been held up by a late crew member. Trapbinder ordered the rest of the crew off. They looked at him funny but, hey, it was his boat. Serod, still in his pajama pants, and Trapbinder, wearing an unfamiliar look of joy, seemed to dance onto the boat as light as angels. The crew watched from the pier in astonishment as Trapbinder pushed the engines to full and sailed out into the predawn darkness. They had little time because in twenty-one minutes the sun would rise. Not far behind, however, was Largent. The police called him after the convalescent home had reported the late night hi-jinx. Whatever was going on, he wanted to consider firsthand the financial implications.

The faster police boat pulled within sight of the Miss Riches close to the spot where Serod had been rescued. The policeman said to Largent, "We have them now. They have no place to go." In fact, they did not seem to be trying to race off. Their boat was idle in the water, rocking gently in the mild seas. Largent and the policeman noticed the two standing on the edge of the deck. It appeared they were going to jump. The policeman picked up his bullhorn and pushed the levers forward to get the boat there before they jumped. "This is the police—" Largent grabbed the bullhorn and pulled the engine to a full stop. "What are you doing?" demanded the policeman. Largent defensively responded, "It's not safe, let's stay here and see—" Largent suddenly stopped his stammering when he realized the deck glowed under a soft blue light. He pushed the policeman out of the way and moved quickly to the side of the boat. They both stared out at some sort of blue orb, like a hovering star, or a luminescent gateway, hanging just above the surface of the water next to the Miss Riches. Then it vanished.

As dawn broke they approached the Miss Riches, but its two passengers were gone. Largent later swore that he had heard the splash and that the inquiry should conclude without further delay so that he could receive his inheritance. The policeman, who had not heard a splash, and who was too concerned for his job to report what he had seen out there, had his men search up and down the coast for the bodies. The search yielded no results. As for the inheritance, Terry had changed his will a few days prior to his disappearance. All his riches were left to an impoverished school in the town where many of the fishermen and their families lived.

Sunday Best

"I don't want to get my Sunday best wet!" Zim petulantly exclaimed to his little brother.

Little brother was very excited about going on the whale watch, but not Zim. When Zim thought of whales, he thought big, messy and wet. He was not an animal lover, except for possibly the roast beef on the dinner table. Zim was handsomely dressed. He liked getting dressed up for the Son. This was not vanity, as it showed respect. The problem this Sunday was the whale watch. There would be no time to change; what if his clothes got wet? His little brother, however, wore a big smile in anticipation.

As they sailed out of the harbor, Zim noticed Mark's Castle. Mark was able to build it because the Son had been good to him. Mark had listened to the message of the Son. If you are good, you will flourish; if you are bad, you will wither. Zim sometimes wondered about little brother. He did not have the necessary respect for the Son. It was a lovely day on the ocean and the whales appeared from the four directions. Some jumped all the way out of the water, landing with magnificent splashes. The people on the boat cheered as the whales said "Hello" with their flappers and tails, snorts and leaps. It was an affirmation, a sharing between mammals, different animals, but also alike. Zim noticed one or two others who were as unimpressed as he was.

As Zim stood there, behind the crowd that leaned out over the railing, an image leaped into his mind and captivated him. It was of millions of plankton, fed by the sun and filling the ocean, The whales sweeping them up with their baleen not only nourished themselves, but also the whole planet! He shook the thought from his head and nervously brushed off his lapels. The whale watching ended, and the boat headed back toward the harbor. The crowd funneled into the cabin, leaving Zim alone on the deck. Out in the quiet, Zim thought he heard the whales talking to him. The boat was no longer in the whale area, yet the ethereal song of the whales filled his ears. Where was this coming from and how could he hear it? He moved closer to the edge of the boat. Maybe a whale was following them. The high-pitched delicate sounds encouraged him to move closer to the water. He leaned out over the rail. The boat hit the wake of a passing ship and lurched forwards. No one saw Zim go over the railing and into the water.

By the time he caught his breath, he knew that the boat was too faraway. He tried a scream, but stopped halfway. It was no use. Zim, however, had faith. He knew the Son would save him. Just like Jonah and the whale, he would be rescued from the savages of nature. It was too far to swim to shore, so he tried to stay afloat in the hope that someone might notice him missing and come look for him. He stared longingly at the tiny houses on the shore. They were the homes of the good people of the Son. He clung to the view of the coastline with its sharply protruding houses; he imagined his hands bleeding as they scraped against the distant gables. It was becoming dark, and he was getting tired; time to slip beneath the waves and sleep.

Splash! What was that? Then there was another splash right in front of him. Zim pulled his head up above the water. To his surprise, he heard chatter, not of whales, but of dolphins! They spoke to him, too, but it was not the airy echo of the whales. They were funny! The dolphins chattered away, occasionally nuzzling him with their snouts. He thought he could see the stars in their eyes. Just as soon as they had appeared, they were gone. Their visit, however, had buoyed him.

The lights along the distant shore seemed minuscule to Zim, a thin line of artificial light separating the vast ocean from an endless glittering sky of stars. Zim had the sensation that each star reached out to him with a crystalline string of light and held him afloat. Back on shore, there was talk of a search party at first light. His parents prayed to the Son to save their boy. He had always been a good boy. Little brother was not worried because in the middle of the night a raccoon had tapped on his window.

Zim began to sink for a second time, but then he felt a warm kiss upon his eyelids. He opened them to see the ocean set ablaze by a brilliant star rising into the sky. It was the greatest of all stars, the sun! As energy ran into his arms and legs, he realized the most incredible thing, that this star, his sun, knew him personally! It was sublime in its power, and yet he held its energy in every cell of his body. The sun was not going to let him flicker into nothingness. Like the whales, the dolphins, and the stars, the sun made him light; it lifted him.

Suddenly there appeared a smile that Zim used to find annoying, but not this morning! Little brother was waving to him from a fishing trawler and his smile shone like the sun upon the sea. When they pulled Zim onboard, little brother remarked gleefully, "You got your Sunday best wet after all!"

Writer Recluse

David felt like skipping along the lane leading to the cabin at the edge of the woods. He inhaled the crisp fall air and listened to the leaves crackle underfoot.

"Oh, man!" he thought. "This is great, my own cabin for the weekend! No work, no kids, no interruptions, just my writing and me! It was nice of Will to lend me his place."

David walked up to the rickety wooden door of the tiny cabin and, as he fiddled with the rusty key, he remembered his online friends, "Hmm, I wonder if Will has broadband? I wouldn't mind checking my Twitster."

He pushed his way in and flopped down on the only chair in the rustic retreat.

"Well, nothing to do here but write. Guess I'll get to it." He opened up his laptop and started typing. He was unaware that he was not alone in the cabin.

"This novel sure is great," he thought. "My friends on Twitster don't understand what a great writer I am."

David typed for many hours, turning on the solitary lamp when darkness fell. As he typed on late into the night, he became sleepy. There was no Twitster to keep him from sleeping!

He stood up, stretched, and looked for the bed. There did not seem to be one. Then he remembered, Will had said something about a mattress in the closet. At the back of the cabin, in a dark little nook, David spotted the closet. A dingy blanket hung in its doorway. He made his way into the cramped and creepy corner, pushed aside the blanket, and screamed, "Eeeewh! What an icky mattress!"

Still, it was better than the floor. So he pulled it out and, as he carried it, about halfway down one side, his hand slipped into a ragged hole. He dropped the mattress on the floor, throwing a sheet, pillow, and blanket on top. He scampered on. He was tired, more writing tomorrow.

As the mattress gave under David's weight, he thought he heard some rustling. "It must be the leaves outside," he thought. As he fell asleep, nothing moved outside. Inside, however, hundreds of eight-legged bodies writhed beneath him. As David started dreaming of friendly agents, big checks from publishers, and compliments from all his favorite writers, the army of spiders exited the hole in the side of the mattress. One by one, they crept onto the mattress, up along David's arm, and across his face. The leader of the arachnids sat on David's nose. Two more scampered into his snoring, open mouth. They attached spider silk to the inside of his cheeks and surfed his snores. In and out they went with the changing direction of the gale winds.

"What do you mean you love my work, but you don't want to represent it at this time?" David heaved up in bed and the surfing spiders flew across the room. The nose-sitter had to scamper quickly onto the top of his head. Upset from his dream, David decided to get a midnight snack. "Agents!" he thought, "What a bunch of spiders!" As David pushed himself out of bed toward the old-fashioned curved refrigerator, not far away inside the small cabin, the spiders on his arm slid off one by one and gathered at the edge of the bed to watch. The spider on his head hung on for dear life.

David opened the door and pulled out some juice. He poured it into a tall glass then reached for the crackers and peanut butter. As he leaned over to spread some peanut butter, the worst thing happened. The spider on his head fell right onto his cracker. Before it could extricate itself from the sticky spread, David clamped down another cracker on top. Squish! He was so busy thinking about agents that he did not notice the spider tendril sticking out from the cracker and wriggling away. Into his mouth and crunch! Then a drink, but wait, before David brought the glass to his lips, he noticed something in it! Once again, he screamed, "Eeeewh!" and commented, "Note to self: trim eyebrows! Some of those hairs are so large they are not only falling off, they are swimming in my drinks!" Having extracted the still jerking spider leg (that he thought his own hair) he finished his drink and headed back to bed.

The spiders on the bed, having witnessed the spider-snack horror, quickly scampered under David's blanket. David hopped on and stuck his feet down under the covers. His toes found dozens of scratchy little legs. "This bed is so dirty, it itches! It's like there are spiders..." He laughed at the thought, "Yeah, spiders, maybe I could write a story about that." He fell back to sleep with the fuzzy little rascals nestled between his toes.

The next day, David awoke refreshed. What a great night's sleep and now for an uninterrupted day of writing. As he absentmindedly pulled on his clothes, his socks and his shoes, he contemplated plot lines and character development. He climbed into the chair and opened his laptop, and there on the keyboard was a spider! David screamed, "Ahhh! A spider! I hate spiders!" He stood up in horror. Lightheaded, he tried to keep his balance, but something seemed to be wrong with his shoe! He had no time to check, as he had to get away from the spider on his keyboard. He staggered through the door and down the lane, falling from side to side and screaming, "A spider! Yuck!"

Back in the cabin, the spiders were happy to see David go. The arachnids gathered around a freshly wrapped catch, about the size of a toe!

Wish Upon a Radio Tower

Tom clasped one hand around a cold steel bar, made sure he had a good grip before letting go with the other, and then felt for something solid with his feet. The howl of the wind in his ears at two hundred feet made even a little breeze sound gale force. At some point going up this gigantic steel needle, an invisible plane was broken, and he entered a world of sky. A place inhabited by birds, airplanes and clouds, and on occasion, radio towers. As the platform was still a long way up, and as he had to pause periodically to reattach his safety hitch, he found that he would often start to talk. At first, he was talking to himself. One day, however, he realized a voice was responding. It was the voice of the red light at the top of the tower. Now he knew this was not a real voice, and that beacon lights do not actually talk, but he played along because it eased his nerves and helped to pass the time during the long climb to the top. The funny thing was, this particular light thought it was a star just like the ones in the sky. Tom thought this was hilarious, but he never had the heart to tell the tower light that it was not really a star.

Today, however, the light was silent. This worried Tom, and yet he had other worries to keep him company on the climb. He had recently run into an old friend, Mark, with whom he had sat for an advancement exam. Mark was now in a government job sitting behind a cozy, warm desk reviewing schematics and, of course, making the big bucks. Tom would have been doing this, too, had he passed the test. Because of a few missed questions, he had been condemned to a career of tower climbing. Still, being a tower dog was never dull, so he did not mind too much, that is until he found out his daughter was sick. He did not have the insurance, or the money, to get her the medical care she needed. This was the last straw for his wife. She had left him the night before.

"Hey, Redeye!" that is what Tom called the light, "Why are you so silent today?"

There was no response. Tom clanged on the ladder and looked up toward the top. The light of day was fading and he was surprised he could not see Redeye's familiar glow. "I hope they didn't have Zeke take you down already," Tom remarked.

"Hey, Redeye, we really have to talk!" he yelled again. "They're thinking about shutting you down. Yeah, no kidding." He listened again for a response, but none came. "See all those midget cell towers dotting the landscape down there? They are going to put you right out of business! You are becoming obsolete, my old friend!" Still, there was no reply. "Even a star such as yourself," Tom laughed, "they are going to pluck you right out of the heavens!"

"Ah, don't take it so hard. We're not finished yet," he added, but Tom wondered if maybe he, at least, was finished. He really could have used a blink from old Redeye, or maybe a reassuring word or two. There was none today, just silence.

As he got up over eight hundred feet, with just one more long stretch of ladder to go, Tom became seriously worried. Not only was Redeye not responding, as it always did, but now it was clear that no light was shining from the top. As Tom picked up the pace, his footing slipped, leaving him hanging by mere fingers. He was tired, and depressed, and even his imaginary friend was not talking to him. The earth seemed to invite him down. "Just let go, Tom. I will take your troubles away." He kept hanging on because he had to see Redeye.

When he pulled himself onto the platform at the top, the horror hit home. Redeye was gone! The whole unit had been removed. He walked over to the place where it had shone for all those years. Tom could not believe it. He raised his hands to his head and, after a moment of disbelief, started to sob. His hands gently embraced the now empty space. A hammering inside his head joined Tom's heart which was still pounding from the climb. It was now dark and the lights on the distant ground spun below. He tried to take a step toward the ladder, but his knees were weak and he stumbled. All the energy in his body, and his life, was gone, except for the despair feeding the relentless drums inside his head. He pulled himself to the edge, tossing his legs over the side. Like a rag doll, he slumped forwards and let go into the abyss. His mind raced madly as he plummeted toward the ground. In spite of his maelstrom descent, something broke through to Tom. There was a red light among the field of stars! As he passed about halfway down, his safety clasp caught a support bar and violently jerked him back, slamming his body into the tower. He hit the steel hard, breaking his arm in two places. There he dangled in the dark and cold, helpless, five hundred feet in the air. The wind howled in his ears. He searched the heavens for the new red star that had caught his death-bound attention. Delirious, his mind clung to it. The red star's glow seemed comforting and familiar. He thought he heard it whispering, "Don't fall! Don't fall! Who else will look for me in the sky, among millions of stars, and know who I am?"

The next night when Tom awoke in the hospital, his wife was bursting with good news. The tests were wrong and their daughter was going to be OK. "And you, Thomas, you gave everyone quite a scare, hanging five hundred feet in the air from a thread. It is a miracle you are still alive! You are lucky they could get you down."

She continued, inquisitively. "You know, Zeke couldn't understand what you were doing up there yesterday. He told me that when he went up to remove the unit the week before, you had already taken it down."

"What?" asked Tom. "I didn't remove the light."

Then her voice turned serious. "Hey, Tom, what do you say we give it another try?"

Tom eased himself out of bed and made his way to the window. He looked toward the horizon and found the red star that had kept him company the night before. He gazed into her eyes before answering, "OK, I'll give it another try, and maybe my wish will come true."

Flash Fiction Stories: Dystopia

Vanilla Frosting Sky

THERE SHE WAS, THE woman of his dreams, surrounded by toes. June would often take off the Cakemakers' boots. There was a glitch in their programming and they did not know how to deal with de-booting.

"June, did you come back on the tube?"

"Yeah, my head's still spinning."

Traveling by vacuum tube was how everyone got around.

"Is it true that there was a sun attack in Baltimore?"

"If there was, I didn't see it!" June replied.

Sun attacks were reported frequently, but Promith had never actually seen one. He had his doubts whether they happened at all. Like most pasteds, he had never seen the sun, just heard lots of scary stories about it.

"No, the frosting above Charm City was thick," explained June.

She tickled some of the Cakemakers' toes as they started to wallhand her. Their big canned smiles pushing closer.

"June, let's lose these pastry clones!"

June got up and was headed for the closest tube, until she remembered Promith's favorite mode of travel and she turned toward the window.

"You're going to fall one of these times, or worse, I will," she remarked with a smile.

"I know, but the tubes give me the creeps. I can never mind-sleep and I get all twitchy when I'm inside one."

"That's what I love about you, Promith. You're not a mind-sleeper. You know, neither am I."

June climbed out the window. She stopped for a moment to take in the vanilla frosting sky. It was filled with spreaders, busy adding layers to the heavens to protect pasteds from the sun. She scanned the dreary skyline. The proboscis tower atop the large central building was currently glowing green for completion hour; it stood in warm contrast to the dull buildings rising out of the grayish omnipresent haze. She hesitated for a moment because of her high elevation, but continued in spite of it. She was convinced that cogency was far better than mind-sleep. She followed Promith down the grooved edges of the building before jumping onto the spongy white ground.

"Hey, Promith, when I was in Baltimore I met this old man, definitely not a mind-sleeper, and he was saying that the sky was once blue and the ground green. I couldn't help but laugh. I mean, a blue sky and green ground? It might as well be red and yellow!"

"Yeah, June, I don't know. He might be right." Promith could not really imagine such bright colors on anything other than the cable network news or, of course, the proboscis tower. He squinted into the gray, the off-white, and the grayish-white that were the colors of his world. "Sometimes I think there used to be colors here. I can't explain it. I just do."

June pulled a flimsy plastic boot from her back pocket, "Hey, look, I still have a Cakemaker's boot!" They both had a good laugh and made mock wallhand gestures.

When they climbed through the window of Promith's unit, on the ninth floor, they were tired, but they refused to mind-sleep. The purple glow radiating outside meant it was the hour of rejuvenation and that the cable network news soon would be going into its overnight mode. Promith's perch was throbbing, indicating it was time to climb on, but he wasn't going to. "Your thing will be wanting you, too," said Promith to June. "Uh-ha," she responded and came over and sat down on the floor next to Promith. She leaned her head on his shoulder and said, "A blue sky, do you really think so?" She smiled, and they rested together. They entered dreams, but they did not mind-sleep.

About an hour later, the Cakemakers arrived. Palms perpendicular, hands in your face. June and Promith instinctively pulled away, but the Cakemakers followed them with their wallhanding. June did not feel like taking their boots off tonight, which was only a temporary inconvenience for them. Promith would have to climb onto his perch to get them to leave. As he was doing so, he noticed June slipping out the window. He smiled at her as she left; she could have taken the tube but chose the window. He loved her so.

Next day, he climbed up his work building and in through the window. His coordinator did not like him entering like this as it called attention to the window. The other pasteds left their indentations, walked to the window and looked at the sky. The coordinator had to herd them back and sometimes the Cakemakers came.

After everyone got back to his or her indentation, June climbed through the window, causing another window-gathering disturbance. She proceeded to the coordinator's shoes. Promith started to laugh. "The Cakemakers will come for sure, June!" he said. "I love you. You are so funny." As June was taking off the coordinator's shoes, she proclaimed, "I want to be a poet, and write about the blue sky, the green ground, and vast areas covered with water." Most of the pasteds did not hear her. Their minds were asleep. Promith heard her, however, and he had a good laugh, that is, until the Cakemakers came. As they climbed out the window, Promith asked about the water, "The old man say that, too?"

"Yes, there used to be great pools of it above ground!"

"Pretty weird. You going back to Baltimore?"

"Yeah, nothing else to do."

They glanced back and noticed a group of pasteds gathered at the window, looking skyward.

"What's it all mean, June?"

"I don't know, Promith. We're just a couple of pasteds. But I'm glad we're not mind-sleeping."

Post-Conspiracy Toast

Kevin, in his pinstripe Brooks Brothers suit, sat contemplating the busy shopping mall concourse. He had hesitated when his old friend from high school had called and requested, through a jittery, cracking voice, this sudden meeting. Over the years, they had only kept in touch via the occasional email and Kevin was never too sure of his friend's actual location or employment status. When his wife asked about him, Kevin would joke, "He's living on the other side of reality." His wife never thought this was funny; she did not approve of maintaining high school friendships. A hand grabbed him from behind, and Kevin reeled around. There he stood, his old friend, Rosor. Rosor's red eyes stared right into Kevin's soul, sending a sudden chill through his fancy suit.

"Rosor! I almost peed my pants!"

"Sorry, man, we don't have much time."

"What do you mean? Somebody slip some LSD into your coffee?"

Rosor considered this more seriously than Kevin would have liked, and then his demeanor relaxed. He smiled at Kevin, "Come on, let me buy the rich banker dinner!"

"Oh, cut that out. I'm not rich." Kevin was, of course, lying. He was very rich. "Let me treat. I helped the best restaurant in this mall get their financing. It won't cost us a dime."

Rosor looked deeply hurt. He humbly said, "I know this great place, just this once, let me pay."

He grabbed Kevin's arm and pulled him around the corner.

"Grape Fizzy?" Kevin asked.

"You've heard of it?" Before Kevin could respond, Rosor had ordered two large Fizzies and a couple of pretzels. "What a ya have on da pretzel?" Rosor joked.

"Put a little mustard on mine," Kevin shot back.

Kevin found a table and two seats. Rosor pushed a pile of change across the countertop to the cashier and then returned gleefully with the food. Kevin took a reluctant sip of his Fizzy. Rosor inhaled his, and ate the pretzel as well. Poof! They were gone. Rosor mumbled something to himself that Kevin thought sounded like, "We are post-conspiracy toast."

"As you know that I have been on the Illuminati's trail since high school," Rosor began.

Kevin nodded slowly, wondering how crazy his old friend truly was, before responding, "At the time, I thought you were just trying to pick up chicks. All you got were some really weird ones."

A barely perceptible smile twitched across Rosor's face. He started to explain, "I was there from the beginning. JFK had to be the matrix of it all. Then there was the spectacle of 9/11. The absurdity of the Roswell weather balloon story convinced a lot of us. Then there were those kids who disappeared in the early 80s! THEY sent them back, or was it forward? Lost in the eddies of time. What about the amazing Nostradamus quatrain about 1999 and the Chinese embassy? And let's not forget our friends, the Reptilians, the Pleiadians, Joan Rivers and the two popes! I mean, I was on top of it all, always one step ahead. Remember how in high school we would sing, in Keith's raspy voice, 'I'm gonna walk before they make me run'? They, with a capital T H E Y, were always behind the curtain, and I ain't talkin' Soviets, nor was Orwell in *1984*. That book was like the Bible to us. Even for you, once upon a time."

Rosor's eyes had grown large. Despite the bright lights in the mall, his pupils were as big as basketballs. Mall security, a policeman, and two men in black suits had gathered about fifty feet away.

"Hey, you want that?"

Before Kevin could say a thing, Rosor had grabbed the barely touched pretzel and swallowed it, and just as quickly drank Kevin's Fizzy. This was getting weird, and Kevin was wondering how to tell his friend he had to go. Rosor, with desperation gathering in his voice, continued. "Now THEY have pulled aside the damn curtain! THEY have broken the unwritten law! How can we play the game anymore? They are now on our side of the curtain. Do you know what that means? We are now, us and THEM, living in the same cognitive space. Whatever his name is, Coldhouse or something, he was the tacit acknowledgement that their game had gotten way out of hand. They had to out themselves! They need us, are us, could no longer not be US. All that information they copied did not give them power. Instead, it has made them transparent. They admitted, because they had no other choice, that they were spying on all of us. In that very moment, they flew the white flag of divine surrender! In that instant, they put all of us conspiracy theorists out of business! No conspiracy can exist in a world where everything is a conspiracy, from our personal identities to our most secret thoughts, from our gas consumption to our favorite shows. No more secrets; no more conspiracy theorists!"

Sweat from Rosor's brow was now dripping on Kevin's expensive jacket sleeve. Kevin pulled his arm off the table. He noticed the men in black heading their way.

"In a world where it is acknowledged by the government that we are ALL spied upon, there can be no conspiracy theorists. Conspiracy theory bureaucratized. There'll be a damn department for spy regulation, the DSR! I, me and my truth-seeking friends, can no longer exist in this world of perfect transparent duplicity! What sort of animal is a post-conspiracy theorist? And for you, and for those who for so long would not look, who refused to see the obvious because their survival instinct told them not to, with this admission, this big confession, the door has closed upon all of you, and you cannot go back. Evah!" As if for emphasis, Rosor dropped the empty Grape Fizzy cup. It took a big bounce and, before it landed a second time, Kevin felt an iron grip on his shoulder.

"Mr.Kevin C. Veritas. Please come with us. We would like to ask you a few questions."

Panic struck Kevin like a pitchfork from hell.

He stuttered out, "Don't you ... don't you want to talk to him?" Kevin pointed to the other seat *but no one was there!*

Indigo's Song

Frank and Tadashi sat surrounded by state-of-the-art technology. Everything money could buy, and alien technology could build, was here in this observation room. In the center was a small two-way mirror, through which they stared at their children, all 99 of them.

"Quick! Wake up! She's doing it again!"

"You're kidding! What have I missed, Tadashi?"

"I just came in and you were asleep. Come on, Frank! You had better hope Dragon doesn't catch you sleeping. The blue light, she's in it again!"

"Alright, stay cool. Start the blocking sequence. We are going to shut her fun down."

The little four-year-old girl sat up in her metal bed. A soft blue light, that was emanating from no visible source, surrounded her. In fact, they were five hundred feet underground. The light sparkled and danced, eliciting smiles from the little girl, joyful hand gestures, and enthusiastic giggling.

"Bring up the frequency. Block the higher frequencies first. We are going to kill this light. It must be transmitted from somewhere, something. No fun for little girly tonight."

"Do you see him? There he is! Do you see him sitting right next to her? He's holding a couple of circular objects. I think they're tambourines! He's giving one to her."

"OK, we are at full power. He is beginning to fade." Frank thrust a victory fist into the air.

"Frank, she is starting to sing!"

Panic came over Frank's face. Cold sweat appeared instantly on his brow. The little girl was singing a pretty song, mostly a collection of ethereal tones. The monitors started to do funny things. The constant repetitive defense waves, tight and rapid at the higher frequencies, and the low and steady programming waves with their wide sweeps, all began to register extreme gyrations.

"Tadashi, look, the heart monitor! They are changing the rhythm of their hearts, synchronizing them to the beat of the tambourines!" The children's rhythmic tapping of the tambourines sent earthquake-like shock waves throughout the compound.

Frank yelled, "Shit! I'm going in there."

"The Dragon won't like it!"

"You know what the dragon can do!"

Frank fumbled with the lock, his nerves getting the better of him. He tore open the door and started running down the row of beds, desperately trying to gain traction on the burnished steel floor. When he was about three beds away, the blue light vanished and the little girl put her head back down on her pillow. Frank hit a bedpost in the darkness. "Damn!"

"Did we catch it on the cameras this time? And, the little boy, he was so clear, more so than last time. The weird thing ... did you notice?"

Tadashi hesitated. "I did. He looked a lot like—"

"Like he could have been her brother!" Frank finished.

"Her brother lives 2700 miles from here," Tadashi commented in disbelief.

All the girls in the room were created with re-engineered genetic material from infant boys. The boys were selected, through a secret monitoring program, for their extrasensory capacity, but girls were made from the material because they were more stable genetically, i.e. as clones they were a better result.

"Well, at least we shut them down." Frank gestured to the monitors that were now registering the normal blocking frequencies.

"I don't think so. Didn't you see? A few minutes ago, these monitors were so erratic it looked like they were playing Jingle Bells! Whatever they— " Recognizing the anger on Frank's face, Tadashi halted in mid-sentence.

"Dragon wants these incursions stopped. They are contaminating the kids!" insisted Frank.

Tadashi was concerned about Dragon, too. Last time Dragon visited he grabbed the coffee cup right out of Tadashi's hands and ate the whole thing, hot coffee and all, while Tadashi stared on in astonishment.

"Look, Frank, maybe these kids should be with their families."

"What? Back with the scum up there in the herd? Their families don't even know they exist! They have so much more here. They can't go back. We are their family."

Dragon burst through the door. "Where is she? Bring 712 to me.Immediately!" Dragon was about twelve feet tall. He had brownish scales with just the slightest hint of red. His eyes were like black holes and his mouth overflowed with teeth. Perhaps because he was a nostril breather, he had earned the nickname Dragon, but he was not really a dragon at all. Tadashi hid his new coffee cup behind one of the monitors as Frank rushed to get the girl. The kids did not especially like Dragon, but they did not fear him.

712 collected herself in front of the beast, who was easily four times her size. He breathed ferociously down at her before demanding, "Stop visiting with your brother!" Tadashi and Frank exchanged a nervous glance. So it was the brother. 712's face was blank until she remembered something and a smile blossomed. "Brotha told me a secra. He say Drago don't like sing." She giggled a little before singing a single ethereal tone that evoked a blue diamond-shaped space in the center of the room. "Drago go! Goo-bye." And Dragon was gone, vanishing into the oscillating blue light. She looked at Frank and Tadashi, who, in contrast to her serenity, were terrified. She said, "I wike you, but yah toys stink! Goo-bye." The light encompassed her, and then she too was gone.

"What'd she do with Dragon?" shrieked Frank.

Tadashi was trying to call Dragon on his cell, but there was no answer. Some of the other girls had gathered at the door. One asked, "Where's Sevenie?"

"She'll be back," yelled Frank, although he knew she would not. "Go back to sleep!" Visibly shaken, Frank collapsed into his chair.

Tadashi walked over to the two-way mirror and, while watching the children return to their beds, commented, "If Dragon and his people can't figure out a few kids, how long can their control last?"

"These kids! It is all just parlor tricks to them," said Frank, trying to explain. "Dragon doesn't fear them. He is just training the best of them to lead the herd. That's all. That's what they were designed for. Don't freak! We're on the right side. Come on! You are funny, Tadashi, afraid of a bunch of little girls. You should be ashamed of yourself."

"It's not the girls I'm afraid of," responded Tadashi. "If Dragon and his kind understand the power of these kids, as they say they do, why can't they shut it down? They are trying to reverse engineer children! When these children play, something incredible happens, something more powerful than even Dragon's planet-destroying weapons."

"Ah, you are nuts, Tadashi!" said Frank. "My money is on Dragon. You don't control half the galaxy by being afraid of a few kids."

"You might be right," Tadashi replied, "but Dragon better learn how to sing."

Foresight

The world's political situation was deteriorating rapidly. Due to wild economic fluctuations, the new globalism had broken down and three competing regions were positioning themselves for a nasty dogfight for world dominance. There had already been dangerously destabilizing military skirmishes. Omega Alpha was located in a no-man's-land at the juncture of the three. Everyone hoped that the discovery of this archaeological marvel might bring peace to a world quickly sinking into chaos.

The explorers soon found out that this was no ordinary place. They determined that the settlement was three thousand years old, built during a time when the Mediterranean was blooming with civilization. They had expected to find a variety of artifacts such as artwork, coins and, perhaps even, written tablets, but there were none of these. The houses were empty except for clay pots. It seemed as if the entire town had gotten up and fled in an instant. The sudden flight theory, however, could not explain all the anomalies. For instance, there were no bones found, or trash sites, or anything to suggest anyone had ever lived there.

The second boat arrived about a week into the project. It delivered the three remaining families, and a big surprise! The intended boat had been confiscated by one of the warring navies, so the expedition had to use a boat that was doubling as an animal sanctuary. After arriving at the island, the gangplank was let down and the animals, as if from Noah's Ark, departed. They were mostly dogs and cats, but also some livestock and a few exotics. The head of the expedition was upset about this, but commented, "Ah well, they are probably better off here than on the strife torn mainland." It was true that animals fared poorly in the disorder and poverty that seemed to be enveloping the world.

During week three, suddenly the order came to return. War was imminent. At 3 pm, they received the following message: Leave Omega Alpha immediately. A nuclear exchange is probable. Return in all haste. Repeat. Return at once.

The puzzle of this strange ancient place would have to wait. Right after the evacuation message, and as a severe storm was bearing down upon the island, there was an amazing last minute discovery. It was a pot filled with seeds! Stored in a cool and dry place, they had remained viable through the centuries. The storm hit with a vengeance. The explorers huddled in the ancient houses for shelter, even the animals came in for protection from the storm.

A few minutes into the storm, it happened. The sky turned a blinding white, as it would under a pointblank nuclear explosion. It has finally come to this, they thought, World War III, the ultimate conflagration of nuclear annihilation. After about ten minutes, it was all over.

When the storm subsided, three went to investigate the condition of the mainland. When they returned, they could barely speak. They reported that all the buildings and roads, all the cities and towns, even all the people were gone. However, the world was not dead. Instead, it was breathing anew, covered by verdant forest and field as far as the eye could see. On Omega Alpha the empty pots were set out to collect rainwater, and the children began planting seeds. The explorers' state-of-the-art communications gear searched everywhere for help, but found only silence.

They began to realize that the town on Omega Alpha was built for someone. It was built for them! Thousands of years ago, an ancient civilization had foreseen this day of world transformation. The ancients knew that Omega Alpha was the nexus around which the world would cleanse itself, if necessary, of the detritus of human warfare, pollution and selfishness. The ancient seers, who possessed the ability to listen to the earth, had known that if the planet needed to enact a spatial-temporal storm of rebirth, Omega Alpha would be the only place spared. In preparation, the ancients had built a survival town. It would sleep in the earth for thousands of years and awaken only if it was needed by their far future descendants. Thanks to their foresight, the town provided a sanctuary from which people could start again. It gave humanity a second chance. A few weeks after the great event, as the enormity of the situation was sinking in, a mammoth cut marble stone was unearthed in the center of town. On it were these words: *Accountability is non-transferable!*

Children of the Veil

THE OCEAN WANTED TO tell him something. Was telling him something. Sensor 15 had to leave soon. He had to return to the entourage. But this was the first time he had seen the ocean. He was in greater awe of it than he was of the Parents or, even, the Naif. Sensor 15 then saw a vision like none he had ever seen before. It was in his head, but he could feel it in the world as well. Three bright stars in the sky in front of him growing in size. He felt lightheaded and weak at the knees. He sat down on the granite rock. It was cool and solid beneath him, but the vision still lingered, confusing him, making him feel lost. Sensor 15 tried to clear his mind, but the pounding waves beneath him would not allow it. He could not forget the three bright stars.

As Sensor 15 came over the hill, he saw the entourage marching down the lush avenue below. He caught up with it and raced past the different types of servers to take his position. It moved with slow, even strides. In front were the Guards, brandishing their weapons, next the Ceremonials. Some slashed the long and thin Sorosee poles, while others steadily beat the wide Sorungo drums. The Sensors were next, gateways to sensation and proud servers of the Parents. Then came the silver hovering orbs of the Parents, the Father on the right, the Mother on the left. They were directly in front of, and never far from, the Veiled Box that housed the Naif. The Veiled Box was followed by more Ceremonials and, in the far back, a couple of Guards protected the rear.

As Sensor 15 caught his breath and settled into his position, he looked at the lower ones at the edge of the avenue. As always, he was repulsed by them. The lower ones lived in the ditches and hovels of the dry, dusty land that stretched out beyond the lush, sacred avenues. They were filthy and savage, spitting food, screaming, lunging through the fences. The lower ones often broke through and the Guards would have to kill them to protect the Naif and the entourage. They would eat servers alive if they could get hold of one and they had little gratitude for the Naifs whose grace gave them life. The lower ones came into being through the process of creating a Naif. Although protected by the Guards, Sensor 15 was extremely afraid of the lower ones. He especially disliked their smell. Today, however, he thought about the lower ones in a way he had never before. He wondered if there was a deeper connection with them than the Parents would tell. It was said that once they had killed a Naif. It was the most horrible event ever. Each year, during the festivities of Virtual World Day, thousands of lower ones were killed to atone for this terrible murder committed many generations ago.

Sensor 15 held his nose and looked away from the lower ones toward the familiar members of his entourage. He felt privileged to be a Sensor, vehicle for the Parents and obedient of the Naif. Below him were the Ceremonials, numbering eight in Sosurat's entourage. They had to wear blinders when the contingent was moving and sleep in the spot where they ended each day. They ate a gruel of rotting meat. The Guards had it better. In Sosurat's entourage there were seven, a strong contingent worthy of such a

Naif. They were well armed with bright metallic crowd shockers in hand, crimson area disrupters strapped to their waist, and two fear-inspiring disingrenades on their belts. They ate fresh blocks of meat and had pads to sit and sleep on. Their minds, however, were singularly fixed and they could do very little besides protect, viciously and to the end, if necessary, the Naif.

The Sensors were the highest order of server. The Parents could not see, hear, taste or feel without a Sensor. Each Sensor was his or her gateway to the physical world. The Sensors gathered for the Parents the sights and sounds of the world, converted them into digital information and transmitted them, by way of an orgotrans located on the back of each Sensor's head, to the Parents. The Parents had not been in corporeal form since long before anyone could remember. They shared a virtual world, drawing its power from the Centerplexes, in which all manner of games could be played with the other Parents. On Virtual World Day, all the orbs would gather for a grand competition. Each Parent had his or her mind, or "being", electromagnetically maintained inside a levitating silver orb. Their virtual bodies hung out in a virtual lounge projected in 3D above the orbs. It consisted of a couch, an over-stuffed chair and a TV. The TV showed the sights and sounds that their Sensors saw and heard. When these were not being downloaded, the TV displayed other Parents engaged in various video games. On either side of the lounge was a portal, the Mother's to the left and the Father's to the right. This is where they would enter the games. The Parents could never die. They were the eternal possessors of the planet. They watched over it from the Virtual World via the eyes and ears of the Sensors. The Sensors were their one link.

The semi-finals were upon the Parents and they were busy preparing. Virtual World Day was not far off and Sosurat's Parents had a chance to make the finals this year. Sosurat's Father had reached the ninth level of Awesome Giuseppe and his Mother currently had the second best score in Warfare Princess. If they could win, or even place in the top four, this would bring great glory to Sosurat the Pure and his entire entourage. They would qualify for the finals at Virtual World Day, and their Naif's entourage would march near the front during the Parade of the Sacrosant.

The Naif was the center of the entourage and of all existence. The eight supreme states were alternated to give the Naif the perfect supportive surroundings. A combination of sound, imagery and ion adjustments spoke directly to the Naif's soul, nourishing his spirit. Each Naif represented one of the eight supreme states. For Sosurat it was purity, thus he was called Sosurat the Pure. But Sensor 15 could not help but notice that their eyes did not express an inner light. They were hard like steel.

Sensor 15 heard the shrill cry of the Naif. Sosurat had cried two times this week. The worst of all times was when a Naif cried. Sometimes this was because a server had dropped the Veiled Box. More often, no reason could be determined. When the cry was heard, blood had to be sacrificed to ensure the Naif's happiness. This was the only time the Naif was ever seen, except on the holiest of days, Virtual World Day.

Sensor 15 was concerned because the entourage had been depleted by two members and there had not been time to replace them. He had noticed that almost without exception the Naif would select for sacrifice the member on the far left of the front line. This was a position he had been fortunate never to have occupied. The choice of position, however, was not his as the Mother always lined up the members for selection.

Earlier, as he was feeding the sensations of the ocean to the Mother, there had been an awkward moment. He had concealed something from her. He did not share with her the vision of the three bright stars. She tried to pull it from him, but he would not let her. It became very strange and uncomfortable. Somehow resistance had found its way into a machine worn perfectly smooth through the years of Virtual World. Eventually the Mother ceased her attempt. Sensor 15 let the rest of his sensations go to her without hesitation. He wondered at his desire to keep the vision from the Mother. What would the Mother think?

The Naif was crying. The Sorosee were slashed three times. The Naif still cried. The Mother elevated herself above the servers and ordered, "Prepare for the selection." As she went down the line, from right to left, Sensor 15 was not, as he usually was, chosen for his third spot. As the dreaded number six spot approached, the one on the far left, Sensor 15 could feel his heart pound. Images of the ocean waves crashed in his memory as he heard his designation, and then his assignment, position six! His mind raced. It was still possible that he would not be chosen for the blood sacrifice. The Naif had sometimes chosen another position, perhaps from the second row, but it was unlikely. Sensor 15, despite his growing apprehension, was, as he always was, awestruck at the glorious unveiling of the Naif. The Ceremonials slowly rolled the electricene canopy back. On red lavender cushions sat Sosurat the Pure in all his benevolent glory. He was the giver of life to all in the entourage. He was a god whose facsimile features and uniform skin guided the world. Although Sensor 15 had seen many selected before him, and most from the very spot he now occupied, he could still feel his love flowing to the Naif. He had the hope that he might not be selected for the blood sacrifice.

Sosurat's eyes moved along his servers, all at attention. In the first row, he moved immediately to Sensor 15's position on the far left but, before nodding his decision, he moved slowly away. Sensor 15's heart was in his throat. He was sure he had been selected but, no, the Naif had moved his gaze away. Sosurat rested his stare on the three spot, the place where Sensor 15 was usually at attention. He stared for a long time and this appeared to be his selection. Sensor 8 stood there in terror. Suddenly, Sosurat moved his stare. Turning again to Sensor 15, without the slightest hesitation, the nod was given.

The rows immediately fell away and four guards grabbed Sensor 15, one grasping each limb. A fifth guard pulled the orgotrans off the back of his head. Blood started to pour down his neck. The lower ones by the side of the avenue could smell the blood and it drove them into a frenzy. The drummers started the slow beat of expulsion. Sensor 15 knew what would happen on the twelfth beat. The back of his head hurt, but everything seemed faraway, distant, as if viewed through a tunnel. Even if the guards let him go, he was sure he could not move a finger. He was frozen in fear; he awaited his end. There seemed to be an interminable amount of time between each beat. Memories flooded his mind. He remembered his orgopreps, when all color, sound, taste, touch and smell first entered his empty mind. His learning of language and his training for service. He recalled his first days with the Parents and the Veiled Box. How he experienced the world for the Parents and how he lived for the Naif. Next he remembered the ocean, and the three bright stars, then the awkwardness with the

Mother. His sensations grew in intensity. He felt the pain on the back of his head more acutely. The smell of the dust kicked up by the lower ones, the feel of it gritty on his skin, the sound of the drums, and the screams of the waiting lower ones. They were screaming for him. Soon they would eat him alive.

Sosurat sat calmly, a contented smile on his face. He always looked very pleased with himself after a selection had been made. The Guards had Sensor 15 at the edge of the crowd and he could smell the stench of the lower ones. He could feel their saliva splattering against his face as they shouted and drooled in expectation. The Guards, preparing for the twelfth drum beat, held Sensor 15 over their heads. There was a flourish of the Sorosee. The Parents eagerly awaited the blood sacrifice.

The blue sky hung above Sensor 15 and he did not move. He was being sacrificed for the Naif. The lower ones would perform one of their functions, that of consuming the sacrificial server. As he got one last upside-down glimpse of Sosurat, whom he had always loved so dearly, an unexpected feeling came to the surface: revulsion. Suddenly he was in the air, light, easy, floating as if he would never come down.

He landed on a mass of tangled lower ones. What grabbed him? Hands, feet, teeth? There was so much screaming, so much commotion. Suddenly, there was the sharp sensation of teeth sinking into his back. A fist landed on the side of his face, dislocating his jaw. The pain progressed with a cacophony of his screams, each second bringing some new infliction to his body. Through it all, however, he found himself wishing for only one thing, that the stench was not so bad. The smell was stronger than even the pain. The patch of blue above him, through a tunnel of endless grasping limbs, made him think of the ocean. As he started to grow numb, he longed for the cleansing smell of the ocean. He wanted to be there again.

All of a sudden, through the now numbing pain, the lower ones started to sway and part. It was as if some force was pulling them away from their blood meal. Sensor 15 noticed a stick. It was electrified, and each lower it touched screamed and moved quickly aside. He saw one sizzled badly, stumbling away in convulsions. The lower ones cleared above him. When he looked up, there was only the still smoking electric stick. There was an arm on the other end of it. It was attached to a body that had two more arms and a large, stubbly face on top. Sensor 15 was not pleased with this turn of events. He was forced back from the half-conscious brink of death into the extremely painful land of the living. He was sure his injuries would not let him live long and yet this lower one had removed from his immediate future the soothing possibility of oblivion.

Sensor 15 managed to fumble out through a broken jaw, "Please. Kill me! Quickly! It hurts. It hurts badly."

The hairy face smiled and mumbled a reply, "I ain't killin' ya. Worked too hard to git ya, besides I got plans for ya. I got big plans for ya. So don't, and I mean don't, go and die on me. If ya do, I'll git ya. Yes, I will, I'll git ya."

Sensor 15 was relatively sure he could not move, but with a slight touch from the electric stick he found himself up and leaning against the three armed man. They moved rapidly away from the still reeling and smoking crowd of lower ones.

Sosurat the Pure and the Parents were disappointed with Sensor 15's blood sacrifice. The images the other Sensors transmitted did not contain any good pictures. The lower ones had not consumed Sensor 15 in a visible manner. The action had moved away from the ceremonial area, off behind some trees. Without actually seeing the dismemberment, the event was disappointing and somewhat unsettling.

The Parents sat in their virtual lounge. The Mother, in her Warfare Princess gear, reclined swinging one leg over the arm of the over-stuffed chair, and said, "Oh well, it is good Sensor 15 is gone. He was defective from the start."

The Father, sitting on the couch in his Guiseppi suit, nonchalantly shot a fireball at the ceiling and commented, "I hope the next blood sacrifice is more satisfying than that one."

The entourage prepared to resume the procession. The electricene sides slowly lowered around Sosurat's angry face.

SENSOR 15 FADED IN and out of consciousness. He could not believe he was alive, even if the pain persistently reminded him. His rescuer, whom he had learned was named Riz, had bandaged him and given him some food and water. Many groups of the lower ones stared at him with curiosity and surprise. They were not used to seeing a Sensor alive in their midst. Many would salivate, some even tried to take him. Riz would not allow this. With a weapon in each of his three hands, he viciously fought off any potential threats. They stayed clear of the large groups. As they walked, Sensor 15 noticed the most odious of things. There were huge caves, holes in the ground, stuffed with the rotting flesh of the lower ones. These huge festering "mouths" gurgled and sloshed as they broke down the copious amounts of flesh stuffed into them. Sensor 15, in a moment of cogency, asked, "What are those?"

"They're a disgrace and you're gonna help us git rid of 'em," Riz said, as they moved on through the heat and the dust.

After several days of walking, they entered the foothills and the masses of lower ones began to thin out. Sensor 15 had regained some strength. He thought back on the bizarre turn of events that had led to his current situation. He had never heard of such an outcome to a ritual sacrifice, although on occasion the final demise of a server was obscured. What he missed more than anything was the giving of sensations to the Parents. He approached Riz and asked if he could deliver them to him, but Riz roughly brushed him away, saying, "We're gonna get ya hooked up with somthin' else. Just hold on for a while, will ya?" Sensor 15 was frustrated by this, but he figured Riz was his new Parent and so he should obey.

As they traveled across some brush, Riz abruptly pulled Sensor 15 through a slim break in the trees. Hidden behind it was a path that curved around a rock outcropping. Riz swiftly led Sensor 15 behind the rocks, up a steep path, along a thin ledge for about ten feet, and then over the top of a hill. On the other side was a pleasant clearing situated around the opening of a cave. In the clearing were several lower ones. One of them began to screech horribly at their approach. "Ah, shut up, Whistles," Riz yelled at the lower one. "He's with me. I told ya all I could git one and I did. His name is Sensor 15. And don't bother him!" Sensor 15 was relieved that Riz knew these lower ones. There were five of them and they crowded around Riz and Sensor 15. They seemed relieved as well. They were happy to see Riz, the more so as he had brought them food. Whistles, who was not much more than a hopping head, with an eye on each side and several delicate plumes that whistled, stopped his piercing screech and was now making inquisitive little cooing sounds. Two massive lower ones, who Riz called Clong and

Clong, had devoured their food and run back to hide in the bushes. SK was almost normal looking, except his arms were so long they had to be kept bent at the elbows to keep them from dragging along the ground. "Where'd you get 'im? Where'd you get 'im?" he asked excitedly. There was one more lower one in the group. Even though he thought he had seen it move when they first arrived, Sensor 15 wasn't sure if it was alive. It was no more than a clump of fur, like a living circle-cake inching along the ground. Riz saw Sensor 15 staring at it and said, "Oh yeah, that's Herman. He don't say much."

That night they had a huge meal consisting of many types of vegetation, not like the flesh blocks Sensor 15 was used to, but a lot more tasty than the mush they had been eating on the journey. Sensor 15 asked for meat blocks, but Riz angrily insisted that none of his lower ones ate meat. Riz had made a huge fire and after dark, Clong and Clong came out of the bushes. Riz seemed to know which giant was which and would indicate one or the other with the slightest inflection of his voice. Their huge features hung half in shadow and half in firelight. SK never strayed far from Riz and attended to his every command. His eyes constantly flitted from side-to-side and his long arms restlessly searched for a comfortable position, never quite finding one. Whistles began to hum an ethereal assortment of harmonics that wrapped the little circle in peace, and also kept the bugs away. And Herman, he was there as well. He never got too close to anyone. Riz seemed the most concerned about his well-being. He stayed barely visible at the edge of the shadows.

Riz told Sensor 15 what he knew of the history of the planet before the lower ones, before the Parents and before the Naifs. He explained that long ago, there were no Mulations (this is what he called the lower ones) and there were no Rulers of Death (this is what he called the Parents, Naifs and their entourages). There was some sort of combination of the two. People had two of most things, two arms and two legs, two eyes and two ears. Much like the servers except they did not serve anyone. They did not need machines to reproduce, but did so on their own. They did not construct life, as the Rulers of Death do, but a being was formed when two entered into a union. This went on for a very long time. Unlike now, the young would grow older, just as their parents did before them. When they were old enough, they would have their own children. There was no need to create Mulations as there was when making the Naifs. The planet was plush and green, not barren, hot and dusty.

Riz went on to explain that people started to neglect their responsibilities and squander the planet's bounty so that the planet was drained of her riches. It was thrown out of balance and a huge war was fought over the dwindling supplies of food and energy. The young people were conscripted to fight this terrible war. The war went on for many decades. The fighting was brutal and many died. By the time it was over, there was almost nothing left for the few who survived.

In despair, the survivors of the terrible war decided they would stop the world. There were not enough resources left on the planet to keep them alive, so they constructed a Virtual Reality world. The only times in their lives that they were truly happy was when playing video games. Now they would enter this world of simulated existence by having their minds electromagnetically placed within orbs. This "new world" would be a place where games could be played over and over again eternally. And for their children, they saved the best of all. They would be made of a "new and improved formula," thus the name Naif, that would keep them young forever. In their biological perfection, all would bend to their will. Like gods, the Naifs would rule the world.

Riz concluded by remarking on why the huge Centerplexes were built. From these, the Parent spheres draw their power, and it is at these locations that the Naifs are constructed to the highest standards. 333 creatures must be made before a pure one is manufactured. The Mulations, of course, are the other 332, destined to roam the planet for however long or short their defective bodies will carry them, or until a reprocessing cart collects them to be turned into meat blocks to feed the servers and the Naif.

"But now the planet talks to us, the Mulations. It yells, "Stop!" It told us to git a Sensor so that the big change can start. Tomorrow, I'll tell ya how ya goin' to help, Sensor. We'll git ya hooked up with somethin' better than those Parents. Now git some sleep," said Riz. Everyone fell asleep and only the crackling fire broke the silence of the night.

Sensor 15, however, did not sleep well that night as SK kept reaching his long arms over and fiddling with his feet and poking him in the side. Riz said not to let it bother him, as SK was just looking to keep his hands busy. "Shine the stars, SK, shine the stars," Riz told him. SK, still asleep, raised his hands toward the sky and started to make minute shining motions. Sensor 15 was left in peace and he finally got some sleep.

The next day, Riz gathered Herman, SK and Sensor 15 at the entrance of the cave. "Now ya follow Herman. He'll show ya where it's at and when ya get there, listen! Ya better be able to hear it because it's been askin' for one of yer kind. I ain't goin' with ya 'cause it shuts off when I'm around. SK will take care of ya if ya need anythin'. Now go!" Having said that, Riz kicked the dirt and walked back toward the glowing coals in the circle of the fire. SK had been given a torch to light the way. Herman was somehow inching, at a good clip, ahead into the cave. SK, with his eyes darting from side-to-side, looked at Sensor 15 and gave him a big goofy grin.

Sensor 15 started after Herman. The cave was much deeper than he had imagined and they went on for some time. With his free hand, SK would sometimes scrub one of Sensor 15's knees but usually he kept it busy by touching all the rocks along the cave's walls. After about an hour, Sensor 15 saw something glowing in front of them. SK, with his long free arm, stopped and pointed to it. As Sensor 15 approached, it became apparent that it was part of the cave. The rock was glowing and emanating a warm heat. A circular symbol was etched into it. Herman had taken up a position right below the glowing rock. Sensor 15 did not know what to think and being alone with two lower ones in such a place was making him nervous. He heard, resonating from all around them, a clear voice saying, "Hello." Although this startled Sensor 15, it had a soothing tone that helped to put him at ease. SK and Herman seemed to be expecting it. "Come. Put your hand within the circle." As he cautiously approached, Sensor 15 noticed, to his surprise, that SK's free hand was perfectly still and that Herman appeared handsome in the light. As his palm and open fingers came closer to the rock, he could feel a presence. He placed his hand on the rock and became connected. He was shocked, not by electricity, but by a rapid flow of images. Millions of images were flooding his mind. This rock had much greater memory capacity than even the Parents! Sensor 15 stood there, overloaded with images. He could not move.

After only a few minutes, Sensor 15 pulled his hand from the rock and hurriedly began to make his way out of the cave. He did not need the torch. SK and Herman followed as quickly as they could behind him. He strode out into the middle of the opening so briskly and forcefully that Clong and Clong did not have time to retreat behind the bushes. Whistles' song abruptly ended on a high note and, turning about, Riz remarked, "What the—" Sensor 15 did not even know what he was about to say, when in a powerful voice, he proclaimed, "You shall no longer put the dead ones into the open pits. The pits shall all be cleansed of the rotting flesh and the flesh burned. In the future, whenever someone dies, they are to be washed, respects paid, and burned to ashes." After saying this, he fell to the ground.

THE NAIFS AND THEIR entourages continued to march through the world. The Parents, as they did perpetually, competed in the Virtual Reality competitions. Virtual World Day arrived, and the entourages began to gather at the Centerplexes. It was quite a sight to behold. The Ceremonials from all the entourages joined together to put on a show of unsurpassed pomp and majesty. Hundreds of Sorosee clapped complex rhythms in perfect unison. The Sorungo beat powerfully in support and all the veils were lifted so that the Naifs could see.

There was also the Great Display of Loyalty by the Guards. They approached the edges of the Centerplex with precision step. An uneasy silence filled the air this year as they looked out over the lower ones. There seemed to be less of them and, stranger still, some lower ones looked on from the hills in the distance. This had never happened before. The Great Show of Loyalty commenced. The Guards fired their disrupters indiscriminately. The lower ones' parts flew in every direction. An occasional hurl of a disingrenade would scatter limbs everywhere. It was a sight to behold. In a sort of hysterical dance, the lower ones not killed would run for their lives until they too were obliterated. In the midst of this carnage, the reprocessing carts went out to retrieve great gobs of heaving lower ones, the dead, the dying and the living. The Guards were showing their loyalty and prowess. They were punishing the lower ones for the day long ago when a Naif had died at their ungrateful hands. They were punishing them for being low and vile. But mostly the lower ones were being punished because they were thoroughly powerless to stop it, crippled by their physical malformations and overpowered by the weapons of the Guards. The Naifs loved this part of Virtual World Day. They all had big smiles on their faces.

Virtual World Day continued with the Parent spheres forming a high circle above the entourages so that the final round of the Virtual Reality games could commence. The Parents prepared themselves at their game portals. Before the final games began, Sosurat's Mother commented to his Father, "Why were there so few lower ones this year? And those watching, have you ever seen that before?"

Sosurat's Father answered, "No, I have never seen such variance in lower one behavior."

"Do you think Sensor 15 is among them?"

"Why do you persist with your questions about Sensor 15? He was a blood sacrifice. He is no longer."

"There was something strange about the day he was sacrificed, as there is today. Perhaps the Naifs are failing?"

Sosurat's Father responded with anger, "Do not question the eternal Naifs. They cannot fail. Their strength has made us rulers of the world. Through them, we will control our destiny forever."

CLONG AND CLONG HAD gotten the word out. Those lower ones with the ability to reason, to feel and to wish (and there were more of these than their malformed physical compilations would suggest) took the word eagerly. They cleaned out the caves and burned the flesh. Those that could, also obeyed Sensor 15's second message: Do not follow the entourages, do not let them collect you for food and, above all, do not eat their blood sacrifices. When Virtual World Day arrived that year, many lower ones did not show up. Others watched the festivities from afar. The lower ones were beginning to see the depravity of Virtual World Day. Although utterly foreign to them, a sense of worth was starting to arise within them.

Sensor 15 had formed a connection with Riz and his lower ones. He felt a warmth, similar to that of the glowing rock, for each of them. Riz said his group was called a "family" and that now Sensor 15 was a part of it. Sensor 15 liked being part of a family.

Each time he would go into the cave, upon touching the rock, the images would flow. He would not know what had happened until he awoke outside the cave and Riz would tell him what he had said. There had been many messages, and each one seemed to improve the lot of the lower ones. Yet Sensor 15 also had a growing awareness of the horrible plight of the lower ones. Physical remainders from a horrific process, used as fodder and food. This was no life to live. After many weeks, the messages stopped. Sensor

15 would go into the cave, but the rock did not glow. Months went by and all of Sensor 15's wounds healed, but still no message. He grew very fond of Riz and the lower ones. They were his family. There was much joy. Still, the pain of their defective physical existence and the horrible legacy of their origins could not be fixed, could never be fixed. Another Virtual World Day approached. There was a feeling growing among the lower ones that this time it would be different. One day, about a week before Virtual World Day, the rock again glowed. When Sensor 15 regained consciousness, Riz was standing over him excitedly.

"Ya said the time of Great Change has come. It'll happin on Virtual World Day. All the lower ones that can are to git to the edge of the ocean." Excitement ran through Sensor 15. He knew this was going to be it. The time of completion. He would return to the ocean. Over the next few days, as Virtual World Day approached, the caves around the world started to emit rarified musical tones. Although far apart, they could all be heard together. They resonated beautiful melodies filled with sadness. It was as if they were singing to the stars.

Sensor 15 stood upon the rock outcropping where he had first seen the ocean, where he had that first thought that had led to his expulsion and his new life. Riz and the others had joined a group of lower ones down on the beach below, but Sensor 15 decided to sit above the sea and watch the sky. As darkness began to fall, three stars were brighter than the rest. He remembered them from the image he was given when he first saw the ocean. He also could remember them from the images that the rock gave him at his last meeting. These were the cleansing stars. They were the harbingers of the Great Change. They would end the wrongs of the current world so that the planet could be new again.

All the images from his connection with the rock started to come back to Sensor 15. They were too fast before, but now they came to him at a pace he could understand. The planet's story was just like Riz's telling of it. The world was once green and lush. A person was not a lower one, server, Parent or Naif. He was all of them, but not split into parts. He lived in harmony with the land. People gave thanks to the planet by having joyful celebrations. But then tall buildings began to arise, and thick smoke raised a curtain to the sky. The lushness of the planet began to fade, the deserts grew and disease increased. Horrible explosions and wars erupted, and seething chaos encompassed all things. After the greatest of world wars, the time of the Naifs and the Parents arose. Their peace was a barren one, their eternity a dead one. The planet was forced to digest the discarded flesh of the lower ones who arose as by-products of the biotechnology through which the Naifs were made eternal. Eventually, it could bear no more. The planet called, with a heartfelt song of anguish and despair, three stars from the sky to heal her wounds.

The stars were coming now. They were growing brighter each second in the sky. Sensor 15 knew, as the lower ones probably did as well, that this would be the end of their lives. It would not be, however, a futile ending, as the deaths of so many had been before. The planet was bringing life back into her fold so that it could begin again, not in fear and pain, but with balance and joy.

Sensor 15 watched the approaching stars all night. Just before dawn, he fell into a gentle slumber. He was awakened by a great shaking. When he looked into the sky, there were only two stars approaching, now extremely bright and clearly visible even in the day. Way off in the distance, red and black smoke flowed into the sky.

He looked over at the entourages. The Virtual World Day ceremonies had not begun. The Sensors, Guards and Ceremonials were all looking at the sky. The veils on the boxes had been lifted and the Naifs all stared as well. They had a countenance, noticeable even from a distance, that Sensor 15 had never seen them wear before. It was fear. They did not enjoy it like they did when they forced it upon others. The Parents were extremely agitated. They sensed their artificial world was about to end.

A profound calm came over Sensor 15. He felt the potential of life. Somehow, things had gone horribly wrong. The planet, however, was strong and just. He was sure that the spirit of the lower ones would inhabit the new world, lush and alive, no longer haunted by the Rulers of Death. A great hum of expectation arose on the beach below. Sensor 15 leaned back and looked at the sky. The promise was being fulfilled. He noticed something move in front of him. It was Herman. He had scaled the ledge and found Sensor 15. They were an unlikely duo, but they had helped heal the planet. For the first time since Sensor 15 had known him, Herman seemed happy. It was as if he had been made whole again.

So that life might once again flourish, the planet was reclaiming her own. The Naifs and the Parents would not be among them. All the servers had left the Parents, and the Naifs, and headed for the ocean. The Parents could no longer see. The giant rocks hurtling towards them had disrupted their magnetic fields, ending all transmissions. The Naifs sat with their veils up, harshly exposed to this last of their perfect days. They looked strangely small and insignificant without their entourages. Sosurat the Pure fell from his Veiled Box and grasped at the ground. He plaintively invoked each of the eight supreme states, but the planet he had never listened to was now not listening to him. There would be no Parade of the Sacrosant today. Sensor 15 almost felt sorry for Sosurat. The Parents and the Naif had never enjoyed life, damned to the perpetual repetition of barren rituals. Their only pleasure had come from observing the contingency of others, an end they somehow thought they would eternally avoid.

The Gung-Gung Tree

THE GOLDEN ORB OF THE sun hung among the sinuous branches of the giant Gung-Gung like a divine ornament in a cosmic Christmas tree. As he said his morning prayers, Liu Zihao, with his straight black hair in a traditional pony tail tied tightly behind his head, and with his work-calloused hands clasped together. remembered his deceased parents. Although having long past, he spoke to them each day. He looked, with his boyish face, that did not accurately represent his nearly fifty years, upon the magnificent tree glowing in the light of the newly risen sun. Punctuating his prayers with bows, he prayed for his younger brother, Liu Bo Cheng. Bo Cheng, was bigger but not taller than Zihao. He was the brother with ambition. He had left for the city several years ago and had become, by all reports, very successful. But Zihao worried about him, so he prayed in earnest. Bowing again, he began his final prayer, for the health and well-being of his village and, of course, for the majestic Gung-Gung tree that watched over it.

The tree itself was a remarkable triumph of nature. It stood well over one hundred feet tall, although no one had ever measured it exactly. Such a mundane action performed on a thing of greatness like the Gung-Gung would serve no purpose but to insult nature Herself. The tree had a divine energy which could be sensed as soon as one saw it, no matter the distance, and indeed, it could be seen from miles in all directions. As to the exact type of tree, there was much discussion which, nevertheless, always remained civil. The Gung-Gung was never a tree to inspire unkindness in any form. In fact, it inspired quite the opposite. It had silver smooth bark, with very few knots, and in many places had distinct orange highlights that would shine brightly in the sun. It also had a blue-green luminescent quality at night. The Gung-Gung had beautiful flowers around late June, much like a Mimosa, but much larger, and its seed packets were silver and shook like marimbas from late fall through winter. It had an immensely wide and solid trunk. It took three people with arms outstretched to encompass it. Growing outward from its trunk came many long and full branches. The children would climb it, but only so far, because in the upper branches one's head would become very light. People would often sit and rest on one of the long and incredibly strong lower branches. No matter the severity of the rain, the tree always provided excellent shelter only allowing a light mist through to those sheltering beneath its branches.

Many years ago, Zihao had walked to the Gung-Gung with his brother and there waved goodbye. His brother often wrote to him with great enthusiasm, telling of the many wonders of the city. He described endless rivers of smooth rock over which self-propelled carts rolled in the thousands, moving many times faster than the work horses in the village. He told of a rocket, taller than the Gung-Gung tree, which he had often climbed as a child, that flew right up into, and through, the sky! He also described boxes displaying pictures that moved of people from around the world performing wondrous feats with magnificent machines. And the parties! The parties he told of were beyond extravagant and, sometimes, were held to celebrate nothing at all! The last wonder he mentioned were the guiding screens that contained ALL knowledge. Everyone had one and could ask it anything, and it ALWAYS had the answer.

    Zihao very much wanted to go see the wonders of the city. He set about saving diligently so that one day he would be able to visit his brother. It took him many months, but eventually he had enough money to go. Zihao always kept very busy and the people of his village had come to depend on him for many things. Before he could go to the city, a friend of his had a daughter who was soon to be married, Soo Si. Zihao felt he should help with the preparations. He did not mind as it was a beautiful cherry blossom wedding. The young bride was adorned in silk and flower petals, and there was much eating and happiness. The whole village danced around the base of the ancient Gung-Gung in celebration. Soon after this wedding, Zihao was helping a neighbor plow his field. When he was in the field, the Gung-Gung caught his eye. It had a message for him: Go to the city now. Time is running out. Zihao made his excuses and prepared to leave. He packed his things hurriedly and got as far as the Gung-Gung, but then the rains came as they never had before. He had to abandon his visit to the city. Before the rains had stopped, Zihao had lent the trip money to a friend so that he would not lose his farm. It was not an easy decision, but he figured in a few more months he would have enough to try again. The second chance was not to come. About a year later, a messenger boy delivered to Zihao the news he had always dreaded. The big city that Liu had loved so much had taken his life. The message did, however, contain some good news. It was from Liu's wife. He had married her just before he died, not telling Zihao as he wanted to surprise him with a visit, one which his unexpected death prevented. Now she was pregnant with his child and on her way to the village!

When Si arrived, Zihao met her under the Gung-Gung tree. This was not a scheduled meeting. Zihao had been listening to the evening under the great tree, as he often did, expecting his new sister-in-law in a few days. She had been fortunate to leave early, however, and so met him under the tree. Zihao knew immediately who it was. He bowed respectfully and walked her back to his house. When she was settled in, he would show her the village. As she unpacked, she handed Zihao a thoughtfully wrapped parcel that was Bo Cheng's. Inside was a carefully preserved leaf, pressed in wax paper, from the Gung-Gung tree. Si said it was his most treasured possession. Zihao carefully re-wrapped it and hurried into his room to put it in a safe place. Soon the baby was born. Si named him Ming. When he was young, he played under the Gung-Gung with the other children, and in the evening he would often go with his uncle to stand by the tree and reflect upon its majestic presence. Si told Ming Zihao about his father and about life in the city. When she spoke of the city to the boy, this worried Zihao. He was afraid that as soon as he was old enough he would want to go to the city filled with wonders, as his father had before him. After he had finished his schooling, he approached Si and his uncle and told them that, although he had known much happiness as a child in the village, he planned to go to the city to make his way in life. His uncle said nothing, but trembled imperceptibly at the news he knew would come one day. His mother bowed respectfully and told him that he may do this if he wanted, but that she was too old to return and would stay in the village. The night before his nephew was to leave, Zihao took out the case with the Gung-Gung leaf. He handed it to the young man. When he opened it, Ming said only one word: BEAUTIFUL. The next day he left early as the sun started to shine through the Gung-Gung. As his heart was unsettled, he took out the leaf and held it in his hand. He could feel the strength of the tree and, even, the presence of his father, in the beautiful leaf. He said goodbye to his mother and uncle and headed for the city.

As Ming passed the Gung-Gung, admiring its beauty, a sudden wind snatched the leaf from his hand. It blew up high, beyond his reach, so he dropped his things and chased after it. The leaf carried on the wind to the river, which lay not far beyond the tree. There the wind ceased, and the leaf alighted every so peacefully on the river's gently flowing surface. Ming sat down on the edge of the river to watch the leaf. As he did so, it turned into one of the carts that did not need a horse. It was shiny and loud, and then many more of the shiny carts appeared causing a great commotion. Ming noticed that the reflection of the Gung-Gung tree in the silvery water of the river had turned into a colossal building that reached into the sky, and the river itself had become a brazen, hard and hot path which no longer curved wistfully, but now shot a glaring line that pierced the horizon. When Ming went back to collect his bags, he paused for a moment before picking them up. He looked at the Gung-Gung, which thankfully had returned to its beautiful form. As he did so, the flowing river whispered something in his ear.

Everyone was surprised when he came back through the door. He announced with confidence that he was not going. His mother and uncle were very happy. He did mention with sorrow that he had lost the package with the leaf. His uncle looked surprised at this. He went into his room and brought out the package with the Gung-Gung leaf in it. Ming immediately unwrapped it, and there was the leaf! Zihao explained that he was going to give it to Ming the night before, but that Ming had gone to sleep before he had a chance to. Ming went to the door and looked at the Gung-Gung standing, as always, by the river. Tomorrow, he said, I will gather another leaf from under the Gung-Gung, and one day I will give it to my son as my father gave this beautiful leaf to me. When he said this, the Gung-Gung tree glowed brighter, and Zihao, Si, and Ming, and his future son, all lived happily ever after.

Wicker Aesthetics

GOOD EVENING, MR. WICKERS, can I call you Samuel?

I think for this interview, Sam is appropriate. Mr. Wickers is an odd thing that I don't think you'd much understand. Sam will work just fine because I can see you're a riverboat man.

A riverboat man? I am not too sure about that. I have been on one or two and, well, I do stay close to the Missouri.

Then you are a fortunate man. I dare say the Mississippi never left my side, although sometimes Mr. Wickers forgets after a glass of champagne or two at one of those high society get-togethers. As I'm sure you know, there is a part of me that never left the river.

If I may ask, how did it happen? How did you remove, like feathers from a cattail, the sights and sounds of your youth?

Oh yes, ask. I will say much what I always say, as those who know me are aware of, and those who have heard the tales about me, well, they are likely to believe anything. My childhood days were erupting in so many directions, filled with bright sunny days at the center of this great country. I could no more have predicted my future at that time than get Huck to put socks on. There was no need to, you see, life was all around me and flowing over at the top. Now it is funny, as of late, I have heard about a fine and fancy library or two, not far from my Hartford home, that at one time thought my books too vulgar for their young patrons. No boy ever had it better than you'll find in the pages of those books. I dare say that sort of thing is what many a young New Englander needs.

Ha, ha, I see your point. But isn't it true that your young characters often lacked parental guidance and many times would engage in flights of fancy far removed from the real world?

You are darn right they lacked parental guidance, and it is a good thing! For they were guided by the insects flying in the fields, and the short, stocky animals roaming the woods, and those odd human counterparts of this wilderness that bumbled through small town society and, of course, the river led them into the heart of every matter.

I have thought on occasion, when etymology and word play take my amusement, that 'Hartford' represents the place where the 'heart has crossed the river' and I guess this applies in my case to my adult years. Whereas Hannibal, he crossed the Alps on elephants in an incredible and unlikely adventure. and I dare say my childhood experiences, in the upspring of life in a Mississippi river town, were not dissimilar.

So, you see, we are not a country that follows the moral precepts of our European ancestors. Oh, now, don't get offended. They are all fine, alright, but what I want to say is that we are a nation of the land, a country built by each other, but placed upon the land. All we need as Americans is the grandeur of nature that God, in His benevolence, has given us to share. These two qualities will keep us on course and protect us through the years, and America will remain the best of places.

Since you mention this, is it not so that in your time, toward the end of the century, you witnessed the Gilded Age, and the push for American industry and money, and even military, to take a larger role in world affairs? And in my time, America is engaged in a world situation that seems dangerously out of control, that seems to require changing everything, even to the point of vilifying where we have been. There are even those that want to return to seeing us in terms of our English colonial days,

Americans are not English. I know, I know, this sounds funny, and I certainly do not mean it as any kind of cultural slur against the English. But as Americans we just have different bones than the English. I mean, we are made differently from top to bottom. The English are the ones who love to meddle in world affairs, sending off ships filled with trouble in all its different forms. I dare say, they were surprised when our forefathers decided they wanted to go it alone. It was hard to tell from across the sea, but after a few generations of basking in the majesty of this great land and, let's not forget, learning from its native inhabitants, there was little of Europe that interested us anymore. God had made our plate full, and it was a new type of life, one free of royal shenanigans.

Now there was something that interrupted my life, a little conflict that tore this country right down the middle. It was especially hard felt in places like Missouri, but without a doubt every American felt it and, I would hazard, many probably still do, even in your time. Now this sort of thing has brought us back, some might say at gun point, to a seat at the European table. Half the time when I find myself at the ostentatiously decorated table of my East coast counterparts, I think I might as well be in one of the fine and fancy royal courts of Europe. For a bunch of Puritans, they sure know how to set a table, and bring the spread!

But Americans are not Europeans, and I dare say, the Europeans who come here stop being European in a very short time, or else they go back, but not many do. Stepping onto

American soil, you are beginning an adventure in a land where nature is immense and woven into the fabric of who we are. There is plenty of space to knock around in, and it all hasn't been organized like those European kingdoms. Sure, there have been attempts to organize it, but most have been just partly successful. Americans are travelers. Even when we put down roots, we still travel around, float down the river, take a steamboat to a new town. Wherever we go in this great land, we meet people just like ourselves, people who share an affinity for this country. It's an unshackled feeling, a sense that we can solve things on our own, if we are decent, and Christian. The rest of the world, I would imagine, will try to involve us in their squabbles, and if American politics has anything to say about it, we certainly will get tangled in a mess or two. But Americans will never be understood by the rest of the world. Hell, they won't even come close, because we have already left them behind, and our interest is here, in America, wherever our two feet can take us, and whatever our two cents can buy, and sure, we can talk about anything all night because we're all kings here, and all peasants, too. Some of us can even play a musical instrument, and that is when you feel the real spirit of this land, the joy and the freedom are irrepressible.

If you might conclude by talking about friendship. Your characters have deep and abiding friendships. Please talk about this a little.

Well, I feel like you are trying to trick me with this last question because, you know, a friendship is a hard thing to define. In my books friendships happen naturally, they arise from the dirt and capture their participants. In fact, upon reflection, I think there is nothing a friendship abhors more than contrivance. Any form of it is repulsive to the situation of finding oneself with a friend. As soon as rules and requirements and church clothing get involved, why that friendship is in shallow water, headed for the sandbar. No, I would guess that friends are mostly friends because they have found a space outside of, or sometimes hidden somewhere within, all of that Becky Thatcher social nonsense. You see, a friend relies on a friend above anything else, no matter how treacherous the circumstances may be, or how shaky the friend's qualifications actually are. He or she understands who you are on the inside and you trust them not to betray this knowledge. Human-to-human is a hard bond to break when it is more than mere pretense. 'Cause it is not about being qualified to be a friend, but more so, it is about seeing the quality in your friend. Sometimes this actually works out, not always, but sometimes.

Well, thank you, Mr. Wickers. I think you have been a friend to many. I can't imagine navigating this world without the compass your books have provided.

Navigating is just floating with a little luck. (They both laugh.)

The Two Million Year Cursmudge

HE SAT ON THE BISECTING ridge of the galaxy. The central ridge, a mere few feet high, hanging above oblivion. It ran the whole length of the Milky Way, a hiccup that could never be flattened. They had waited for Godot. He had been by three times. The rabbit that was late for a very important date. He came running up to the ridge, stopped and said, "Oh my!" He then sat down and chatted for a while after he realized he could never be late. Tide and time not only waited for no man, but for everyone else. The ridge was much like that six inch drop at the edge of the sidewalk. Some call this the gutter, but if you have ever sat with your butt on the sidewalk and your sneakers six inches below on the street, you know how time stops. These two edges share an attitude.

As a two million year Cursmudger, you can live as many lives as you like, but you are always connected to your spot on the galaxial ridge, or ripple, and it makes you just a little off. There are never a lot of people who choose such a destiny. But for those that do, it is the ultimate hang, satisfying beyond anything. In fact, that is its very point. You see, if everyone went about in sync, all the time, no one would know anything about the universe, or chess, or flowers, or any particular thing. All this would be there, of course, but the awareness of it would not. So the Cursmudgers come in with contrary vibes, not mean, or destructive, or asinine, just contrary.

And when they interact, they bring the tension, the difference, the space necessary for everyone, and everything, to have the big "Uh-huh!" moment. Which I am sure if you have had it, you know it to be positively exquisite, if sometimes a tad unsettling.

Life as a Cursmudger, however, is not always easy. You never truly fit in, never can completely lose yourself in that wonderful spinning galaxial sync, because you are sitting on the sidewalk that crosses the entire Thing. You are on the spatial anomaly whose exception proves the rule. You sit on a quantum ledge where place and movement, location and speed, come together. Some might think this two million year stretch of awkwardness undesirable, or tedious, or lonely. It is true that few choose it. It is completely optional. Yet there has never been a Cursmudger who was not sad to leave. There is much to do, besides the always satisfying hanging out. The most popular activity is taking a stroll among the stars. There is no rush. Two million years is a good amount of time, and if a walk takes ten or even one hundred years, it does not matter. Because in the end, two million years on the galaxy's third rail is but the wink of an eye. And from then on, wherever your spirit might wander, you will always recognize another Cursmudger when you are lucky enough to encounter one. You can reminisce about the sweet years perched upon that curving string, that great bow, which plays the rarest tones in the Milky Way.

Last Run of the Day

LATE IN THE AFTERNOON the bright glare of sun on the snow had fled. The world was cold and blue. The skiers were set in dark relief under the giant steel chairlift girders. Hank came flying off his last run down the hardest trail. He was exhilarated. He wanted one more run, but was not sure if there was time. He noticed there was no one standing between the ropes to the lift. His heart sank. But wait, the chairs were still moving, and the attendant was still there with shovel in hand. He flew up the line. The attendant was surprised at another customer so late. His friend yelled from behind, "Hank, going to do one more?" Hank heard himself convulse, "Last run!" He was going to pull out of the loading area and wait for his friend, when suddenly he felt a hard hit below the knees. He fell back into the chair and was away. He thought the lift attendant had been a little hard with the chair delivery. The chair swung down, free of the pad. His stomach seemed to stay behind when the chair headed skyward. Lightheaded, with legs still tingling from the impact of the chair, he started his ascent into the growing shadows. He turned around to see if his friend had hopped on the chair behind him. He had not. He appeared to be arguing with the lift attendant as the attendant pulled a rope across the entrance to the pad. "Ah, that sucks!" he thought, "Guess for the last run I'll be going solo." The gears from the first girder jolted him forwards with an unsettling Grrrr! Clunk, clunk! Grrrr! Clunk, clunk! He turned around to face the top of the mountain, a long line of empty chairs in front of him. Maybe there were two people, seven or eight chairs in front of him. It was difficult to tell in the lessening light. "Hope they don't shut this down before I reach the top," he considered. A gust of wind whisked the snow from the top of the trees below. Hank hunkered down into the collar of his ski jacket. The ride had just begun.

The first part of the ascent had a modest incline, as it traversed the wide, flattish slopes where all the trails met at the bottom. The shadows on the trees were growing long, and he did not see any skiers below. Just some snowplow bomber, caked in snow, emerging from the easy trail. He saw another skier, who was obviously very good, flying down the expert trail. Hank wasn't sure, but it looked like they would reach the convergence of trails at about the same spot. The snow-plower was mostly in shadow. There is no way the expert could see him. If they both maintained their speeds, it would be a near miss. Hank leaned over the edge of his chair a little too far to take a closer look. The chair, having only one rider, tipped downwards toward the snow below. "Come on, snow-plower, a little faster," urged Hank. The snow-plower emerged onto the main concourse. Finally, the expert could see him. But it was too late. It would take a miracle! The expert veered to his right. The snow-plower turned and saw the cannon ball barrelling towards him! His only reaction was to lean backwards. His right ski lifted and the expert's ski went under it. The sound of fiberglass hitting fiberglass crackled sharply through the cold afternoon air. The snow-plower spun like a top, both his skis releasing. He tumbled down the slope, limbs waving in all directions, before coming to rest several yards away. The expert had no such luck. He had lost one ski, as it had jammed into the snow under the snow-plower's ski, thus pushing him into the air. There he flew, one ski on and one ski off, floating through the blue light of the late afternoon, like a ballerina perfectly executing a jump in Swan Lake. There was, however, no way this could end well. After a few moments of antagonizing expectation, he landed at high speed on one ski. He found his balance. Was he going to pull it off? Hank was getting ready to pump his fist in congratulations. Instead, he bit into his cold glove. The wipe-out was horrendous. One for the books! The expert went tumbling down the hill, doing pinwheels in an attempt to stop, but having no success he disappeared in a ball of snow. Hank wondered if he would be OK. He looked for the snow-plower, but the chair had moved too far up the mountain for Hank to see anything more.

CHALING, LING, LING, LING! His chair was pulled past another girder. He leaned back. Wow! That collision was intense. He was feeling tired from a full day of skiing, his bones ached a little. Maybe this extra run was not such a good idea. The chairlift had left the bottom of the mountain and was now moving up a steeper incline, pulling into the late afternoon shadow of the mountain. He closed his eyes, all of a sudden he felt the tension on the cable weaken and, as it sagged, his chair dropped several feet. He threw his arms out, grabbing at the sides of the chair. This chair isn't stopping, is it? Hank was familiar with chairs pausing on occasion, usually when someone fell trying to get on, but there was no one behind him! He looked back down the cable line all the way to the lift hut. He noticed a singular puff of dark, gritty smoke sailing into the sky. "What the hell?" he whispered to himself and turned nervously around. Tentatively, he stared at the hulk of the dark mountain. "It won't be long," he said to himself. "Just a few seconds and we'll be on our way." And just like that, the lift started back up. Clunk, clunk, clunk, it went by a large girder. Hank started to say to himself, "Not a prob— " when the forward motion dropped out from under him. His chair swung to and fro, like a rocking chair in the sky beneath the creaking cable. "Oh shit!" he said. "Will this ride never end?" He was currently traversing a long plateau. The girders were set far apart, and the chair sagged quite low between them, maybe only fifteen feet above the trail. "Well, I guess I can jump from here," he thought to himself. Resting his cold chin on his hands, he said out loud, "Maybe I should," and then less loudly, "maybe I should." As Hank stared at the empty trail below, a lone skier pulled up nearby. It was sort of odd, the two of them not twenty-five feet apart and no one else around. Usually, there is not much talk between lift-goers and the skiers below, but this situation seemed to demand a few words. The skier below, who Hank could tell was an older gentleman, wore a dark pointed hat, navy blue parka, and had long, thin skies that looked like they had skied right out of the 1940s. He commented, "Did they shut down the lift and forget you were on it?" Hank, who had a similar sense of humor, normally would have laughed, but somehow he could not bring himself to laugh this time. He closed his eyes for a moment, searching for a response and not finding one. When he opened his eyes, the skier was gone. Hank twisted in the chair, searching for him, but there was no trace. He was headed for a warm drink in the lodge. A cold gust of wind turned Hank back around in his chair. "Forget me?" asked Hank, "No way! I think they have some way of checking who the last rider of the day is." Hank was not sure what that was. He looked up at the riders in front of him. With their distance and the late afternoon light, they were hard to see.

It looked even colder up there, and they were over much steeper terrain than Hank. At least I am not up there, he thought, at least I am not up there.

After about ten more minutes, that seemed like thirty with Hank seriously considering jumping the twenty-five feet to the snow below, the chair began to move again. "OK, here we go," he said tentatively. The chair moved forwards, slowly gaining speed. Hank leaned forwards somehow thinking this would help. Perhaps it was for encouragement, or maybe he was leading the way, whatever the reason it did not seem to work. The lift never regained its normal speed, but instead ground forwards at a an uneasy half-speed. After a few minutes, Hank realized the futility of his posture, and sat back in the chair. CLUNK, CLUNK, CLUNK, another girder went by. The pitch of the terrain then took an unholy turn upwards. As the chair moved into the last and steepest part of the climb, the cold, dark mass of the mountain closed in around him. There were no trails below anymore, just the service cut for accessing the girders. Much of what was below were jagged boulders, gnarled pine trees and any bush that could find a place to grow amongst the rocks. Over one hundred feet in the air, Hank stared at the rocks below. With the sun behind the mountain, the water from the mid-day melt-off started to freeze into a threatening shade of steel blue. Hank decided he would not look down. "If only this thing could go a little faster!" he said loudly. "Faster ... faster ... faster ..." his echo replied, scaring him half out of his seat. He laughed and said, "You gotta love echoes." It was then that he remembered the Sun Tower! It was by far the tallest girder on the way up. His friends had labeled it the Sun Tower because it reached so high the sun appeared to rest on top of it. Even on sunny days, Hank felt a little queasy passing this towering girder. It seemed to guard the top of the mountain like a gigantic Roman soldier. The fear, in spite of the cold, moved swiftly through his limbs. He tried to swallow but there was no saliva in his mouth. "No big deal, no big deal," he reassured himself. The people in front of him had just cleared it and were now heading toward the last few girders before the mountain top disembark ramp. "If they can do it, I can do it."

Shhhsssk, shhhsssk, shhhsssk. Another girder passed, but why the weird noise? That was not a hearty clunk, clunk, clunk. "What happened to my clunking noise?" He turned and looked back at the girder falling back behind him. It was ice! Ice was forming along the wheels over which the cable moved. It must have been the prolonged stop, and the slower movement, combined with the deep cold of the late afternoon. There was one more girder between him and the Sun Tower, but he had the horrible feeling that the already slow-moving lift, was moving even slower! No, it couldn't be. He tried to reassure himself. He was anxious and maybe freaking out a little, so his agitated state probably just made him think that the chair was slowing. Shhhsssk, shhhsssk, shhhsssk. The hole in his stomach opened into a bottomless pit. The lift was slowing, alright, and next stop was the Sun Tower. There was no sun above it now. Frozen shadows framed the imposing hulk. "OK, so we are going to have another little break before we get to the top," he said slowly to himself, while wondering why this shit always happened to him. His friends would all be having a warm drink in the lodge, laughing and telling stories about the day of skiing. Hank was sure none of them had a day like the one he was living through. They all probably thought he had gone home early. His siblings and parents would be back at their ski cottage walking around in their heavy wool socks and putting together some sort of hearty dinner. CRAAACK! What the hell was that? It must have been a branch far below. The wind had picked up pretty good by now. It made a constant low whistling sound. Hank could not tell if his chair was moving anymore. It hung way out in the space between the towers. It was either moving very slowly or not at all. It did seem that he inched closer to the Sun Tower or, again, was that just his mind playing tricks on him?

He started to consider the possibility that his situation might become a lot worse. There were many possibilities. None of them too good, He was already frozen through. His chair slowly started to move up toward the girder wheels. It felt like the thin wood slats of his chair were mere stalks of hay and that he might be carried away by sheer vertigo in the frigid air, the jostling wind, and the menacing height above the jagged snow-covered rocks below. As he got closer to the wheels, Hank could see all too clearly, "Holy crap , look at the ice on those things!" It was then, about twenty feet from the Sun Tower, and about two hundred from the ground, that his chair stopped. It swung backwards and downwards! He hugged his ski poles for dear life. Eventually, his chair stopped swinging, and everything became very still. Hank felt alone in the world like never before. It was cold, everything a gray-blue shade that seemed darker than night. At least at night there were stars. No matter where he looked, he could find no solace. The contracting gray sky above, the massive frozen tower just feet away, the distant ground far below. He closed his eyes for a moment and found himself in the awkward position of not wanting to open them again. He felt encouraged to keep them shut by that slimmest of chances that this might all be a bad dream. He did not want to open his eyes and confirm that it wasn't. He tried, but they wouldn't open. So Hank negotiated, "Alright, I know, this is what we will do, I will turn my face toward the sky, so that our precarious altitude won't be so overwhelmingly apparent." Hank adjusted his head for a look toward the ramp at the top and, sure enough, his eyes opened! And what did he see?

He wasn't sure. He had to shake his head and look again. There was a skier in a bright red ski patrol jacket! Hank shook his head again. The skier was still there. He was skiing down the access trail beneath the girders, but he wasn't just skiing. He was vadeling! Hank had never seen anything like it. It was so incredible that for a moment he forgot his situation. He strained in the low light to see this vision better, and he almost leaned out too far. "Whoa there!" he pulled himself upright into his chair. This skier was vadeling over rocks and ice, at a good clip, perfect posture, with his eyes straight to the front at all times. Hank had seen some great skiing, but this took the cake! As the skier got closer, he wanted to caution this "God of the Ski Patrol" to take it easy. When Hank saw people skiing like this, it usually ended in a massive wipe-out, and that was the last thing he wanted to have happen now. There was nothing he could do, however, except watch and pray. The vadeler continued to come flying down the access trail, skis clicking in the air. As the skier moved closer, Hank could see he had on a white hat, black skis, and yellow fiberglass ski boots that shone like the sun in stark contrast to the dismal frozen landscape. He also carried with him a sense of light and warmth. Possibly even hope. Hank wondered if he was seeing things, or maybe this was just some crazy person skiing the access trail in the near darkness just for kicks. Hank breathed a sigh of relief. The ski patrol vadeler stopped, almost directly below him, at the bottom of the Sun Tower. Without even taking a moment to catch his breath, he stuck his ski poles into the snow and stepped out of his bindings. What was he going to do? He wasn't going to climb the Sun Tower, two hundred plus feet straight up, with no safety cords, and in his ski boots! Yes, he was!

Hank could not believe it. The rather thin metal ladder built into the side of the tower would be a next to impossible climb in the summer with appropriate footwear. Hank stared in amazement as this intrepid individual, or perhaps "daredevil" was more appropriate, climbed the tower in a direct and unyielding fashion, much like he had vadeled down the access trail. He brought with him one of his ski poles, looped around his right hand. He probably could see Hank as he climbed to the top of the tower, but when he arrived at the top he was all business. He immediately took his ski pole and started chopping at the ice in between the cable wheels. His first thrust was a little too hard, and one of his boots slipped off the ladder. He pulled it in, looking down for a moment, before proceeding more cautiously. Hank did not move a muscle. He did not want to distract this "Ski Patrol Super Hero" in any way. The ice had become fairly thick and did not give way easily. Hank was sure that the vadeler could knock it loose if anyone could. Just as he was thinking this, a large piece of ice cascaded out from between the wheels, disappearing into the gray light below. Several seconds later a crackling, like breaking glass, rose up from the trees indicating that the ice had landed. The ski patrol guru immediately headed down the ladder. Hank could not blame him for not giving him the thumb's up. Hank searched the cable wheels as best he could in the low light. They looked clean now. He figured it would take vadeling dude about fifteen, or maybe ten minutes, at top speed to ski down the mountain and inform the lift operator that the cable wheels on the Sun Tower were clear. Incredibly, the ski patrol climbed down the ladder in much less time than coming up. Even though this was common sense, Hank was no less impressed considering the slippery circumstances.

    Hank's chair lurched forwards. The lift was going again and at regular speed. CLUNK, CLUNK, CLUNK. He passed the Sun Tower and heading to the last stretch before the ramp. He quickly turned in his seat, hoping to see a last glimpse of vadeling-dude headed down the access trail. He wanted to wish him well and to see him ski one last time!. But, no, he was nowhere to be seen. Probably over the first ridge already, or maybe cut back to a trail. Either way, he had got the lift going and Hank was very grateful for his intervention. When he turned back around, it was time to throw up the bar and prepare to disembark from his conveyance of peril, to which he felt he might actually be frozen. He hopped off and skied down the ramp. The top of the mountain attendant was waiting at the end of the short ramp. "Want a ride back down?" he asked, pointing to the empty chairs swinging back and forth and headed toward the bottom. "It's getting pretty dark." Hank could not help but glance one last time at the Sun Tower before responding, "What did the folks that got off before me do?" The attendant gestured to the top of the trail. Two skiers were pushing off, headed down the mountain. Hank smiled and responded, "I'll stick with them on terra firma!" The run down was uneventful. The moon had come out and, with it shining on the white snow, it was not difficult to see. Hank considered trying some vadeling, but decided against it as he was not at that skill level yet. When he returned home, nobody was interested in what had happened to him during his last lift ride of the day. Someone did grumble that he missed dinner. He didn't really expect anyone to understand, but he would remember that ski lift ride and, on more than one occasion, decide to skip the last run of the day, opting for a hot chocolate, instead. As for the vadeler, Hank often looked for his shiny yellow ski boots when he saw the ski patrol. He would never forget his incredible skill and focus, but he never saw him again. He wanted to say "thank you" but perhaps, mused Hank, real heroism does not need one.

Acknowledgments

I WOULD LIKE TO MENTION a few inspirational people. Rita and Nancy, my grandmother and my mother; Harvard "Skip" Knowles, one hell of an English teacher; Hiram Kato, philosopher and weapons expert; Neal Rockett, childhood friend and fellow music lover; Chris Giddings, he lived life to the max; Julian Benello, whose battle cry was, "Keep on with the French toast!"; Baker and Josephs, who taught me grammar and Twain; Shirley Atwell, my mother-in-law and editor of the union newspaper. Also, the #amwriting community, an indefatigable group of writers; my fellow captive boarders, whom I met upon the rolling deck of the battleship Exeter; my Hamilton-Wenham friends, many of whom enjoyed a ride in the red bomber; my fellow booksellers, with whom I worked in the trenches and, of course, my wife and my son, for the shared laughter and the many adventures! Plus, my cat friends, Comet, Frodo, Daisy, and too many others to mention. I have the cat food bills to prove it! Oh, and I don't want to forget, Loker and Winthrop, the mischievous twins from whence this all sprang!

About the author

JASON BEGAN LIFE IN a red American Foursquare not far from the Boston Post Road. As a young teenager he had his spiritual awakening in Asbury Grove. In tenth grade, he was bundled off to a Latin school on the banks of the Squamscott River. After this, he cleared his mind in Ireland where he was blessed by a visit to the Valentia Madonna statue. Later, he earned a MARS degree, Master of Arts in Religious Studies, by wrestling with the dialectic on the wrong side of the Charles River. As a young man he managed bookstores and renovated an Antebellum Italianate farmhouse in rural Maryland. From his backyard he could see Big Round Top and he frequently visited Gettysburg, Antietam, and Monocacy. When the bookstores began to close, he moved west. In North Dakota, he experienced what a house sounded like at 21 below when it "popped". In Arizona, he attended a Hopi ceremony on Second Mesa where clowns climbed down out of the sky and joked with him. He currently lives with his family in a Gordon-Van Tine bungalow in a hamlet filled with trees and surrounded by prairie.

Also by Jason Sullivan

Yuletide Zingle
Death by 9 Iron
iRapture

Milton Keynes UK
Ingram Content Group UK Ltd.
UKHW031207111124
451035UK00006B/618